BY THE SAME AUTHOR

What a Body!

They Died Laughing

How to Do Practically Anything
(WITH JACK GOODMAN)

Love on the Run
(WITH JULIAN BRODIE)

Mother
Of Her Country

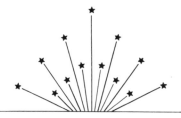

Mother
Of Her Country

A Novel by

Alan Green

RANDOM HOUSE

NEW YORK

Copyright © 1973 by Alan Green

All rights reserved under International and Pan-
American Copyright Conventions. Published in the
United States by Random House, Inc., New York, and
simultaneously in Canada by Random House of
Canada Limited, Toronto.

Library of Congress Cataloging in Publication Data

Green, Alan Baer, 1906–
Mother of her country.
I. Title.
PZ3.G81788MO [PS3513.R435] 813'.5'2 73–5056
ISBN 0–394–48350–2

Manufactured in the United States of America
First Edition

Aside from passing reference to certain historic figures and to an organization which gazes respectfully back on them, none of the characters or institutions in this fiction exists. To make reasonably sure that no real names had inadvertently been used, diligent research was required. For help with this—and for many other favors—I'm indebted to Stanley Crane and his associates at the Pequot Library in Southport, Connecticut.

★

The events of this story occur in 1972 when, in most of these United States, social value was still considered redeeming.

Mother
Of Her Country

1

Rupert Hayes was the only book publisher in New York who had ever gone to Damascus College or, possibly, heard of that school. Which was the sole reason that he happened to be interviewing Laura Conroy.

He glanced again at her brief résumé. Born: Ludgrove, Ohio —June 1950. That made her twenty-two. Last month. Without looking up, he tried to visualize her as she'd entered his office. She hadn't seemed any older than that. Maybe a bit younger. Not as mature as the Bennington sophomores—and they couldn't have been more than nineteen—who came looking for intersession jobs. Or, perhaps, it was that they were often from metropolitan areas and this girl looked small-town. Whatever *that* meant. Now he glanced at her. She sat forward on the edge of the leather chair, her feet primly in front of her, heels touching. More than a little tense. No make-up. But none of them seemed to use that very much. At least, not to show. Slim. Maybe five feet five. Ash-blond, long, straight hair held partly back by a bit of ribbon. Rather pretty, in a shy, serious way. If the résumé hadn't said "Ludgrove" and if he hadn't known Damascus, would he have thought small-town? Maybe not. Yet—innocent. That was it. She looked innocent. How outmoded!

He went back to the résumé. Ludgrove High School '68. Top 10 percent. Editor, *Ludgrove Spectator* (Lit. Mag.). Member Ludgrove Drama Group. Swimming Team—1967–68. Runner-up Southern Ohio women's low-board diving championship. He tried to remember her standing figure. Slim. Gymnastic.

Damascus College '72. Magna cum laude. Major: English Literature. Minor: Creative writing. Editor, *The Damascene* (Lit. Mag.). Extracurricular: Short stories (unpublished). Four feature articles in the Cincinnati *Enquirer*.

"Do they still have the Theatre Society at Damascus?"

"Yes, Mr. Hayes."

"You didn't go out for it? You did in high school."

"No." She seemed to check herself from saying more.

He pretended to be still studying the résumé. Conroy . . . Conroy and Cincinnati. The combination almost rang a bell.

"Did you take the Junior European semester? They still have it, don't they?"

"No. I mean yes. I mean I didn't go." This time she seemed unable to check herself. "I wanted to. But—" She smiled. "This is the farthest I've ever been from home. Alone. I've gone with my folks to the Southwest. And the national parks."

She did have the All-American look. Scrubbed. He liked it. But you saw it all over the world nowadays.

"What does your father do?"

"My father?" She seemed surprised that the subject had come up. "Oh, he's in banking. His bank, really."

He felt almost apologetic. "I hadn't meant to pry. It was just that . . . when you said you wanted to study in Europe, but—"

She bobbed her head with rapid understanding. "It wasn't a question of affording it. It was . . ." She hesitated and he didn't try to rescue her. "It was—well, like not joining the Theatre Society." He made no effort to erase his inquisitive look. "I mean, they were doing different plays than we did in high school. My mother liked me in *Our Town* and *You Can't Take It With You*. Things like that."

"And weren't they doing things like that at Damascus? We did *Life With Father* in the fifties."

"Oh. They're doing other kinds of plays now. Pinter and Brecht. They even did *The Balcony*. You know, Genet. There was an awful fuss."

"Really? Who made it?"

She look at him wide-eyed. "Why, Mother of course."

Conroy. Cincinnati. "Your mother isn't Jessica Carroll Conroy, is she?"

"Yes. I thought you knew. I mean, I was sure you must have heard of her."

He studied her quietly. "Miss Conroy. Laura. There isn't anyone in publishing who hasn't heard of her."

Laura nodded.

"Is this your mother's idea? Does she want to plant you in publishing?"

"Oh no, Mr. Hayes. She was against it. She didn't even want me to be alone in New York. And she definitely didn't want me to get into—you know, a lot of publishing houses—most of them."

"No. I don't know. Aren't we like most of them?" He motioned to the offices and corridors of the rest of William Simmons & Sons beyond his door.

"I'm sorry, Mr. Hayes. I said that very badly. But, you see, you were founded years ago. Why, you've published Hawthorne."

"So has everybody else. He's in public domain." He rose, went to crammed shelves behind his desk and found a book. "We published this, too. And you know what your mother thinks of it."

She took the book he was offering her. *Consenting in Private.* By Priam Wendell. She began to turn its pages. "I've heard of him. I haven't read him."

"Not enough people have. Hardly any, really. Though your mother seems to have encountered it. Or vice versa."

"I know," said Laura. "I read about it in her Bulletin. She doesn't like it."

"She calls it unmitigated filth."

Laura stopped at a page and read for a few moments. "Is it all like this?"

"Like what?"

She frowned, searching for words. "Impressionistic, I guess. Obscure. It's hard to know what he's saying."

"Haven't you ever heard Priam Wendell?"

"Heard him?"

"He reads his poetry. Mostly at colleges. Hasn't he been to Damascus?"

"Maybe. No, I never heard him."

He pulled open a drawer of his desk and searched out a file of clippings. "These are for his latest book of poetry." He pushed the file toward her.

She picked up half a dozen clippings and scanned underlined passages. "Do *you* think he's this important?"

"Yes."

"Some of these papers, I mean little magazines"—she was looking again at the clippings—"I've heard of. But who are these critics?"

"They're modern poets. Very modern."

She turned back to *Consenting in Private*. "This isn't poetry."

"It's a prose poem. In the form of a novel."

She flipped pages. "Why does Mother—? I don't see anything filthy."

"It's about incest. Between two dizygotic twins. In a womb." He studied her. "Does that shock you?"

She slowly shook her head. "No. It's a funny—I mean odd—idea. Why did he want to write about that?"

"Because he wanted to write about how our selves—the different selves in each of us—are both separate and joined—reject and love each other. Being a poet, he found a metaphor."

She seemed puzzled and turned more pages. "I'm surprised Mother understood this. It isn't her kind of reading." She looked up. "Or mine, either. I like clarity."

"Maybe your mother read a review. In a few big magazines

the reviewers made cracks about the scene and the action—
womb is a pushover for bad puns. Look. Even if it isn't your
kind of reading, take it and give it a try. Then let me know
what you think of it."

"As a sort of test for a job?"

"What kind of job do you want? Your letter just said you
wanted to get into publishing." He lifted a defensive hand.
"Not that we have any openings right now . . ."

"I'd take almost any kind of a job as long as it might lead to
maybe being an editor—an assistant or junior editor whatever
you call it."

"How's your typing? Do you know shorthand?"

"I can type well enough, I guess. I typed all my things at
school. But I don't know shorthand. And I don't want to be
stuck in a secretary's job."

"Maybe you wouldn't be. Lots of people who make it in
publishing—editorial, publicity—they start as secretaries. My
secretary reads unsols in her spare time."

"Unsols?"

"Unsolicited manuscripts. First readings. Later they may
become junior editors, or get into some other division."

"But I haven't the time. It takes months to learn shorthand."

"What's your rush? You're barely twenty-two."

"But I only have two months. And more than a week has
gone already."

"Why only two months?"

"Mother didn't want me to come here at all. I pestered her
until she agreed to a short trial and let Dad stake me to just
enough to stay that long at a hotel—the Barbizon. You know
it?"

"Umm. Ladies only. And if you don't connect somewhere
in two months?"

"Then I'll have to go home. Take a job. In Dad's bank, I
suppose. And, I guess, get engaged. There's a young man in
Ludgrove I've dated." She shrugged. "But I want to make good
in New York."

8

Rupert Hayes looked at her for a long time. Then, putting the clipping file away, he said, "Would you like to hear Priam read?"

"Oh, I'd love to. Is he going to?"

"He'll be at the YMHA tonight."

"Oh. Is he Jewish?"

"I don't know. Does it matter?"

"No. No. But when you said YMHA—"

"They have most of the good poetry readings in town. You might enjoy it. And, if you'd like, you could meet him afterwards. My wife and I are having a few people in. We'd be glad if you'd come along." He smiled at her. "Like to?"

"Yes. I would."

Editors of New York publishing houses who do not commute have a tendency to live on the upper West Side of Manhattan, in the less cluttered sections of Greenwich Village, in Brooklyn Heights and the Park Slope area, and a few of them, on the middle East Side. All are relatively high-crime areas, which is almost certainly a coincidence.

Rupert Hayes's apartment was on Riverside Drive just below Ninetieth. Laura went up in a crowded elevator, jammed against a couple she'd sat near at the YMHA. The door to the apartment stood open and a few people had already spilled out into the hall. She allowed herself to be pushed along through a foyer and into a medium-sized living room. Beyond it was a study, the bar and, through a large window, a spectacular view northward to a distant, light-strung George Washington Bridge. Still moving with the crowd, Laura found herself propelled past the bar to where Rupert stood in a little group. Later she had cause to reflect on her unresisting entrance into and through the throng. It seemed symbolic of the way she'd almost sleepwalked into the telescoping situations of the days which followed.

Rupert was talking to a tiny, middle-aged, mousy woman. He broke off and welcomed her. "Hello, Laura. Glad you could come. Enjoy the reading?" He looked down at the other woman. "Nadia, this is Laura Conroy. Laura, Nadia Norse."

The woman said hello and Laura tried to remember where she'd heard the name. To Rupert she said, "He's fascinating. The way he recites his words, I felt I was almost understanding his meanings."

Behind her a man said, "Priam's poems are like a beautiful woman—meant to be felt more than understood."

Rupert said, "Laura Conroy, this is Max Levin. Max, get Laura a drink. She's after your job."

Nadia Norse said to Laura, "Watch him. He sounds like an MCP."

Max Levin steered her toward the bar. "What are you drinking?"

She looked at the cluster of bottles. "Maybe a little bourbon."

He started to put ice in a glass. "Bourbon? You don't sound Southern. Middle West?"

She nodded and said, "With a lot of ginger ale, please."

He pretended astonishment. "Ah. A virgin!"

She blushed and Max tried to remember when he'd last seen that happen. He handed her the filled glass.

"Thank you. What's an MCP?"

"An outmoded term. Male chauvinist pig. Nowadays, girls just call us shits."

She looked at him unblinkingly.

"Well?" he asked. "Don't you?"

"I don't know—*I* don't."

"Then you accept male supremacy."

"No-o-o. I just don't like it." She sipped. "I mean the word."

"What's wrong with it? It has a great lineage. The Old English *scitan*, the Middle Low German *schiten*, the Indo-European *skheid*, the—" Max paused as a young man put an arm over his shoulder and said to Laura, "Max has never recovered from the *OED* going into a cheaper edition."

"What's wrong with citing precedents?" demanded Max. "You bastards do it all the time."

The young man ignored him and said to Laura, "I'm Marc Holland." She saw a thin, dark young man with unruly hair. He looked a little bit like Ralph Nader, but with a strong hint of humor in his eyes.

"I'm Laura Conroy."

"I know. I saw you at the reading and asked around until Rupert told me."

"Do you work for his company?"

"In a way. I'm with a law firm that represents some publishers."

"That must be interesting."

"Usually no. Usually it's reading manuscripts for libel, invasion of privacy, that sort of thing."

"Oh, don't you go to court—you know, witnesses, juries?" She blushed again, tying the 1972 record for the upper West Side. "I guess I've been seeing *Perry Mason* reruns."

"Sometimes I get into court. Assisting one of the partners. Only it's not like *Perry Mason*." He grinned at her. "Although I once helped cross-examine your mother." Laura looked startled. "Rupert told me," Marc explained.

Max said, "Who's your mother? Oh . . . *that* Conroy. What's the old—What's she like?"

But Laura asked Marc, "Why was she in court?"

Marc Holland glanced at her still nearly full glass, turned

to the bar and began to make himself a drink. Over his shoulder he said, "Mrs. Conroy was testifying against *The Dirty Macbeth.*"

Laura was indignant. "*Macbeth* isn't dirty. We studied it a whole semester."

"Well"—Marc turned back to her—"this was a different version. A Tabard Press paperback. I doubt you studied it."

"I never heard of it. Why was Mother—?"

"This edition was the original text, just as Shakespeare wrote it. But it had been interlarded with very erotic stage directions."

"And very funny ones," said Max. "I edited it."

"But I thought you worked for Mr. Hayes's firm," said Laura.

"I do. Three days a week. I'm a sort of semi-free-lance. The other two days I do editorial work for a couple of small publishers. Tabard's one of them."

"And you wrote the stage directions?"

"No. Just edited them." He preened himself. "Oh, I added a touch or two. Like making the witches dykes."

Laura looked startled and confused.

"Dykes," Max repeated. "According to the *Dictionary of Slang*, probably from *hermaphrodite.*"

"Max," said Marc, "you should write a basic work on the philology of the obscene. *The Ribald Linguist* you could call it."

"Or *The Lingual Ribald,*" said Max.

"But I still want to know," said Laura, "why Mother was in court."

"Americans for Clean Entertainment was trying to get *The Dirty Macbeth* banned," Marc explained. And added, "They lost, of course."

"Why 'of course'?"

"Because the court properly wouldn't consider the directions apart from the total text. The text is great literature, the directions were imaginative and funny, hence entertainment of redeeming social value."

Laura was clearly unsure of the point. "But if the entertainment was dirty—"

"But if the dirty entertainment was healthily enjoyable by adults."

"Who says dirt is healthy?"

"Who says it's unhealthy?"

"Lots of people. Mother's taken me to A.C.E. conventions."

"They can say anything they want in their conventions, or anywhere else. But in a court of law they have to prove the book—or the play, or the picture—is guilty of unhealthiness."

A short, thin, ascetically bearded young man came into the study. Laura recognized him as Priam Wendell. He didn't look quite as small as he had on the YMHA stage. A woman, plump, tall and with masses of coiled strawberry hair, was leading him to the bar. "Hello, Marc, Max," she said, "you both know Priam." She glanced pleasantly at Laura.

"Laura Conroy," said Marc, "this is your hostess, Jenny Hayes."

"I'm glad you could come. Priam, this is a friend of ours— Laura Conroy."

Priam took Laura's hand and looked searchingly at her. Then he turned to a languid girl in a white, almost Grecian dress who had trailed him into the study, but she put a friendly hand on Max's arm and veered toward the window with him.

Laura blurted to Priam, "I enjoyed tonight. You read very beautifully."

"I like to—" Priam started to say, when a loud crash from near the window made them swing around.

The girl in white was drifting back toward the bar. But no one was looking at her. The focus seemed to be on someone who was painfully trying to rise from the floor while another man, red-faced, was being restrained by Rupert. The floored figure made it to his feet and turned out to be Max holding a handkerchief to the side of his face and his nose.

Priam said to the girl in white, "What happened, Moira?"

The girl said, "That man hit Max. He thought Max insulted me."

"Had he?"

"No. Max said I looked like the Immaculate Conception and the man—he's drunk—hit him. Max was on the floor calling the man pissed and muttering about it coming from the Middle English *pissen* and the Old French *pissier.*" She drifted away again. Jenny was leading Max toward a bathroom, Rupert soothing the fuddled hero toward the foyer. In the study and the living room beyond, there was a moment of embarrassed silence. Priam made himself a drink and moved with Marc and Laura to the big northern window. They were held by the distant, lovely view. Priam shook his head in admiring wonder and Marc said, "Not much like home."

"Not like either of them," Priam answered. He turned politely to Laura. "Are you a New Yorker?"

"No. A small town—almost a suburb. Of Cincinnati. New York is new to you, too?"

"Yes," said Priam, "except as a visitor. This is Marc's town."

"True," Marc said. "I've lived here since I was a kid. But I know Priam's country. Both of them." He saw Laura's questioning look. "Priam's a Vermonter. Only, now he lives in Provence." Laura nodded as though she fully understood, but her eyes were still quizzical. Marc continued. "He and Moira have a farmhouse in Drôme—that's a *département* not too far from Avignon."

Laura bobbed her head a little more surely. *That* she could place—almost. Exiled popes and a nearby city of artists. Something about Cézanne. And Van Gogh. And somewhere else near there a high Roman bridge. A full-color page in a book —a high school book? A college text? One of those. Not a book at home. There weren't many books there. Her eyes left the window and scanned again the floor-to-ceiling shelves on every wall of the study.

Rupert, alone now, was coming toward them. "Sorry about that little fracas. Chap had had a bit too much." He chuckled. "Imagine punching Max—and the guy isn't even one of his authors."

"Actually," said Priam, "I think it was a rather pretty compliment. Immaculate Conception. And to an Irish girl. Quite poetic." He glanced at Laura for confirmation.

"I don't know," she said, "I'm not Irish."

Rupert said, "Laura found hearing your poetry clearer than reading it."

"That's why my recordings outsell my books. Anyhow, I write to be listened to."

"Maybe so," said Rupert, "but I admire readers more. Listening is a lazier thing to do—"

"—and cuts into your book sales," said Priam.

"True. Nevertheless, I think the ear pays less attention than the eye. Maybe because the eye is nearer the frontal lobe, where the real thinking is done."

"But," said Laura, "when he"—she looked at Priam— "when you read from your novel, *Consenting in Private*, I didn't understand that too much better than when I tried to read it. I'm not sure I know what was happening in the part you read tonight."

"The twin embryos," said Priam, "were making love."

Laura asked, "And talking to each other?"

"No, just thinking. It was an exchange between embryonic minds."

"Then why couldn't they have been talking?"

"Not the way they were making love."

Laura turned from Priam to Marc to Rupert. As though waiting for one of them to explain.

3

In the cab on the way to her hotel, Laura asked Marc about Moira.

"He found her in Ireland. They've been living together for a couple of years."

"Is she a poet, too?"

"She's a weaver. Abstract tapestries."

"Will they get married, do you think?"

He shrugged. "I doubt it. It isn't their style." He looked down at her curiously. "Why? Do you think they should?"

"N-o-o-o. Not necessarily." She thought about it. "There was this couple in Ludgrove—she'd been in my class. They lived together, like a lot of the others. But they planned to go on that way and never get married."

"And what did you think of that?"

"I don't know. I guess it seemed awfully strange then. It doesn't seem so strange to me now. Of course, they couldn't go on living in Ludgrove. They moved to Cleveland."

"It's better in Cleveland?"

"It's bigger. Doesn't that make a difference?"

"You'd be surprised how small Valréas is."

"What's that?"

"It's the little town near where Priam and Moira live—between Vaucluse and Drôme."

She sighed. "There's so much I don't know about. Like living that way and—"

"You mean unmarried?"

"I didn't mean that. I mean like Val—what did you call it? —places like that."

"Valréas."

"Yes. And living like that, too. I mean, between Ludgrove and Damascus . . . A small town and a small college. I guess I mean small-minded." She reflected. "I remember once when a magazine editor was lecturing there. I went to hear him. He was talking about strengthening the U.N. Mother was furious that I'd gone. She said he was implanting Communist ideas."

"Was he?"

"I don't know. That's what bothered me. How was I supposed to tell? I mean, they don't teach you how to tell in college."

"It's hard to teach how to think about things. It's much easier to teach what others have thought." The cab slowed and came up to the hotel entrance. He helped her out. "Let's have dinner soon. I'll call you. Okay?"

"Yes," she said, "I'd like that."

When Laura's phone rang two nights later, she answered it eagerly. "Hello." Her voice was happy.

"Laura!"

"Oh. Hello, Mother."

"Have you gone out of your mind?"

"No. Why? What's the matter?"

"Matter! You've disgraced me. And yourself."

"Mother. What are you talking about?"

"I'm talking about your name in all the papers—and about what you've been doing."

"But, Mother, I haven't been doing anything. Except looking for a job. What papers?"

"Every paper Nadia Norse writes for."

"Nadia Norse?"

"Don't pretend you don't know her. Evidently you were at a party with her. And she knew you'd been to that Priam Wendell's pornographic recital."

"Oh. Nadia Norse. I thought I'd heard her name, but I couldn't place it."

"Well, she's placed yours. Right in the middle of her gossip column. And in over two hundred newspapers."

"But why would she write about me? We just said hello when we were introduced. It was at Mr. Hayes's place. Rupert Hayes, the publisher. He and his wife—"

"I know all about it. And so does that Norse woman. She loved mocking me through you. Twice she called you Jessica Carroll Conroy's daughter. What ever possessed you to go to hear that man read his filth? And at the YMHA, at that!"

"But Mr. Hayes suggested it. And he went to Damascus."

"I don't care where he went. He publishes obscene literature. Didn't the A.C.E. bring him into court for it?"

"Yes. But you lost. You couldn't prove it was obscene."

"I think I know just a little more about obscenity than any of those New York judges. Anyhow, I'm not going to argue with you. I didn't want you to go to New York. I let you persuade me. Now *this* has happened. You're to come home at once."

"That's not fair. You agreed to two months."

"But we didn't agree to your going to the YMHA and listening to Priam Wendell and consorting with a publisher who attacked your mother."

"He did not attack you. You attacked him."

"And with good reason. I'm not going to discuss it. You're to come home."

"I won't come. Not till my two months are up. And not then if I can get a job."

"I think you're forgetting that I'm your mother."

"And you're forgetting that I'm twenty-two."

"But still a child."

"I'm finding that out. That's why I'm going to stay here and grow up."

"Just what do you mean, 'grow up'?"

"Everything. I'm going to find out about things. Like about modern writing and little French towns and why it's all right for two nice people not to get married. And why a man who never saw me before called me a virgin."

"But you are. You still are—?"

"Yes." A long pause. "But, Mother . . ."

"What?"

"Don't expect miracles."

"—and there are other things I could do. I might find a cheaper place to live and maybe a roommate. I might get a temporary job in the evenings. A job in a store maybe. Like a bookstore that keeps open late. Some of the girls in the Barbizon do that. It leaves the days free for job hunting. Not that I've needed much time for *that* so far."

Marc picked up his wine glass from the checkered table-cloth. "How many publishers have you seen?"

"Really seen? Not just leaving my résumé with personnel? Rupert Hayes. Nobody else." She twisted the stem of her own glass. "Maybe there's something I'm not doing. I've answered ads in the *Times*, and Mr. Hayes lent me *Publishers Weekly* so I could answer ads in that. But nothing happened. I ran an ad in the *Times* the other day. So far, nobody's answered. Now I've got one coming out in *PW*."

"What about employment agencies?"

"Sylvia—that's Mr. Hayes's secretary—gave me the names of several that specialize in publishing jobs. I've been to them."

"And?"

"They said the same thing Rupert Hayes did. You know, shorthand and typing. But I don't have the time and certainly not the money for that now." She looked at him candidly. "Mother's just dying for it to run out."

Marc said, "I've talked to several people in our clients' shops. They don't have anything. But I've had one thought. Tabard Press. Ever hear of it?"

She started to shake her head, then seemed to remember. "I've heard of it somewhere. Didn't you mention it the other evening?"

"Maybe I did. Yes. *The Dirty Macbeth.*"

"And isn't that where that man—what was his name—Max Levin works part-time?"

"Yes. One day a week."

The waiter had been removing their plates. "For dessert," he said, "we got nice zabaglione. Also rum cake, spumoni, cheese . . ."

Marc looked at Laura questioningly. "Just coffee, please," and Marc ordered two espressos.

"Ever hear of Lincoln Snaith, Senior?" he asked.

She shook her head. "Does he run Tabard Press?"

"Far from it. He operates a medium-sized publishing house in Los Angeles. Started it after World War II. Just in time for the Joe McCarthy period. And that's the sort of thing he publishes. Very right-wing. Mostly nonfiction. He started out with *How FDR Tricked Us Into War.* Then he did *How Truman Gave Away China.* His latest is *The U.N.—Strangler of Freedom.*"

"Mother has that one."

"I daresay. Anyhow, when Snaith's son came out of college about ten years ago he took a job his father offered him. He thought he could reform his old man. Or, at least, balance the list with some less reactionary things. It took him three years to find out that he couldn't and another year to decide what to do. Then he came to New York and started Tabard Press. He picked up a few young novelists and very quickly lost a big piece of his shirt—he was operating with money from his mother who had left the old man when Snaith was in high school. Then he did some things that broke even and actually made a few bucks. A couple of early ecology books, a paperbound on the protest marches. And a line of offbeat fiction also in paper." Marc started to add something, then seemed to change his mind. "Anyhow, I had lunch with him last month before he went to the ABA—the booksellers' convention. He said something about wanting to find an editorial type who'd done some writing and was enough of a beginner to do odd jobs. Would that interest you? You've written, haven't you?"

"Yes. Stuff for the school paper, some short stories. What kind of writing does he want?"

"I'm not sure. Do you have samples of your work?"

"Yes. That's why I picked on publishing—I like to edit, and write—they *do* write in publishing, don't they?"

"Sure. Publicity, advertising, jacket blurbs, catalogue descriptions. What about your reading?"

"I've done as much as possible. The Ludgrove library has all the classics and quite a bit of modern things. In college we read a lot but not *very* new things—not like Priam's poetry . . . But editing the literary magazine and writing those things—that was the only job qualification I had, and it seemed to lead more to publishing than to anything else." She relaxed with a rueful sigh. "At least, it seemed to promise a way of getting out of Ludgrove."

He motioned for the check. "Let's get out of *here.*" He glanced across at her. "Come up to my place for a while. We can't talk very well in the Barbizon lobby. And they won't let me above the first floor."

6

"So then," said Marc, "We came back to my place and talked. After that, I took her up to her hotel."

"And what," asked Jenny Hayes, "did you talk about? Surely not more about getting her settled in New York?"

"No. I figured it was about time to talk about me."

"Hah!" Rupert went over to the bar and poured more brandy. "The brilliant years at Harvard Law? The bright future at Weaver, Beach and Ellmann? I'll bet you laid it on."

"As a matter of fact I did. Then, when she went back to the john, I remembered that snapshot of Roz and me at St. Maarten—it's still stuck in the mirror."

"So—did she ask about Rosaline?"

"I told her. Told her it was all over."

Jenny looked up at him across her snifter. "Is it?"

"Yes. It is now. For sure. But you still haven't answered my question. Why am I so drawn to a little girl from Ohio—who doesn't know a think tank from a singles bar?"

"Maybe just that. Maybe she's the first girl you ever met you can tell all about it to." Rupert looked at Jenny, who smiled her agreement, put down her snifter on a coffee table and added, "Just as she's the first probable virgin you ever met. You can, er, tell her about that, too."

Marc laughed. "That's something else that's bugging her."

"Being a virgin?"

"Being called one by Max. Seems she asked for a drink and Max accused her."

"What was the drink?" asked Jenny.

"Maybe what she had before dinner last night. Bourbon with ginger ale."

"Oh," said Rupert. "Still, that isn't *always* a sign."

"I thought a Tom Collins was a surer indication," Jenny reflected. "Especially for summertime virgins."

"So now," said Rupert, "you're sending her to see young Snaith."

"She's going there day after tomorrow. I reached him this afternoon."

"And he has a job in editorial?"

"Seems to. Said he'd be glad to see her, and not just as a favor to me."

"But what kind of a job could he have for a girl with no experience? His house doesn't get that many unsols. His receptionist can probably read them between phone calls."

"I know," said Marc, "but when I asked him, he was vague. Just wanted to know if she'd written. And when I said it was mostly school-paper stuff and rejects he didn't seem put off."

"You don't think," asked Jenny, "it has anything to do with his Solus Books?"

Rupert snorted. "Now, what could a girl like Laura do with those?"

"Well," suggested Jenny, "she could read them at night. Just what every Barbizon girl—"

Rupert interrupted. "We know. We know." He turned to Marc. "Will she call you after she's seen him?"

"She said so. I'm sure she will."

"Let me know. I'm curious."

"Day after tomorrow," Jenny murmured. "Why not bring

her here for dinner that evening? I'd like to get to know her better, anyhow. Then maybe I can try to answer your burning question."

Decades ago, New York's publishing industry was clustered below and around Union and Madison squares and on Fourth Avenue, which had not yet been elevated to Park Avenue South. Some of the industry, distinguished houses included, still lingers there, but many firms long since invaded Park and Madison avenues, and more recently the new steel-and-glass structures on Third Avenue and on what, if you're from out of town, you call the Avenue of the Americas. If you're a New Yorker—and, especially, a taxi driver—you still call it Sixth Avenue and wonder what the hell they're digging up toward Fifty-ninth Street *now*. A few small publishers have found less expensive space in midtown by renting in old six-story, one-time brownstones in the upper Forties and lower Fifties especially between Fifth and Sixth.

One of these was Lincoln Snaith, Jr's., Tabard Press. The elevator, added at some time after the building had gone commercial, was a tiny, automatically controlled cage. Laura found herself in it with a tall, thin girl so wanly emaciated as almost certainly to be a high fashion model bound for the top-floor photographer's studio.

Laura squeezed out on the third and found herself in a

cramped and cluttered outer office. One wall was filled with a disorderly array of carelessly shelved books. In front of the shelves, a double gooseneck lamp on an old fashioned gate-leg table inadequately illuminated a small imitation-leather sofa and a straight-back chair. On the other wall, behind a low railing, a very pregnant young woman sat before a monitor board and read a bound manuscript lying flat and open before her. When Laura entered, the girl looked up and waited for her to say something.

"Mr. Snaith—I have an appointment."

The girl continued to look at her.

"Please tell him it's Miss Conroy."

The girl flipped a switch on the monitor board, waited a moment. "Miss Conroy for Mr. Snaith . . . Uh huh." She flipped the switch back and said to Laura, "He'll see you in a few minutes." She jerked her head at the sofa.

Laura crossed to the bookshelves. They held an odd and jumbled assortment. Most were titles she'd never heard of by authors unknown to her. Some appeared to be novels. Most had subtitles suggestive of nonfiction about the environment, population control, natural-food diets and new ways of hand-crafting. Almost all bore the Tabard imprint on their spines. A few were paperbacks with hard-to-read titles climbing up their bound ends. She saw other paperbacks lying on the table face up with easy-to-read titles. She picked one up. *The Lucky Pierres: A Phallic Gallicsy.* Curious, she started to read a passage, turned with greater curiosity to another page and went on at some length. She closed the book wonderingly and looked again at the cover. It certainly was a Tabard Press publication, and above the imprint were the words A SOLUS BOOK. Her eyes returned to the table. Other books were similarly imprinted. She put down the first book and picked up another. *Helen's Awakening or The First Time She Saw Paris.* She opened this one, read, blushed and—involuntarily—giggled. Still reading in the same passage, her eyes widened with astonishment. She turned the page and went on reading, breathing a little more rapidly. She took a step back toward the sofa as if to sit down, appeared to think better of it and remained standing next to the table. She was quite lost in the book when, for the second time, the pregnant girl said, "Mr. Snaith will see you now."

She moved through the open arch out of the waiting room, down a short corridor with a few offices on either side, toward a right turn at the end. Beyond the turn she was facing an open office and a youngish man who must have been the tallest she'd ever seen. He was standing behind a desk and in front of a window over which an open-slatted Venetian blind was drawn. She was dimly aware of other furniture as she crossed to him and put her hand into his enormous offered palm. He was not only the tallest but also, by far, the thinnest. She wondered for a wild instant if he could be related to the emaciated girl in the elevator, but she, in a hunger-struck way, had been handsome. He was just plain homely. His blond hair needed blue eyes; his were brown—as far as she could tell from down there where she was standing. His bony nose jutted abruptly from his pinched face. His mouth, without being at all well formed, was smiling across a jutting jaw. He looked somewhat like a genial moose.

He waved her into a seat next to his desk and folded himself into a swivel chair, bracing his feet against an open drawer. This brought his knees well above desk level.

"So you're Jessica Conroy's daughter."

"Yes. Marc told you?"

"Umm. Ever work before?"

"Not really. Just some volunteer summer jobs. Charity offices."

"And you want to get into publishing?"

"Yes. Very much. I'll do anything. I can read—my English Lit professor said I had very good judgment. I've written, in school—and out of it. I think I could describe books. Marc said something about catalogues and the descriptions on jackets . . ."

"Tell me about your writing."

"Well"—she moved closer to the edge of her chair—"I like to describe things. People. And crowds. Like at football games, how they sound and, you know, look and act. And old houses and landscapes and— I've written lots of essays about books, not just book reviews for school, but things I just *had* to write after I'd read a book I liked. Would you like to see some of it?" She reached into her flat little case and offered him a thin sheaf.

The door behind her opened and a male voice said, "Oh. Sorry, Linc. Didn't know you were busy."

She turned around and saw Max Levin in the doorway.

"Hello," he said. "You were at Rupert's the other night."

"Yes."

"Well, I won't bother you. I'll haul my ass out." He began to close the door, hesitated and opened it. "From the common Teutonic *arse,*" he said, "and the Old Frisian *ers* and the *Old* Teutonic *ars-oz.*" He closed the door.

Snaith skimmed quickly through the papers, pausing once or twice to read a paragraph. "Ever try fiction?"

"There's a short story, very short, on the bottom."

He leafed until he found it and began to read. After a couple of pages, he looked up. "Can you run a monitor board?"

"I once did. In the Ludgrove Red Cross office. During their drive."

"Think while you were doing that you could read unsols, too? We get all kinds."

She thought of the Solus books on the waiting-room table. "I'm sure I could. *All* kinds?"

"Yes. From engineering books to popular sociology to erotica."

"W-e-l-l. I don't know a lot about *all* those subjects."

"You wouldn't need to. You'd only have to know if the manuscript were written well enough and interestingly enough to warrant passing it on to an editor."

"And would you want me to write anything about them?"

"A short description, if you're passing it on. With a word or two about how enthusiastic or doubtful you are."

"I'm sure I could do that. I could do more than that. More writing I mean."

"You'd have to."

"Yes?" She watched him expectantly.

"Do you know our Solus line?"

"Those paperbacks. Out in the waiting room."

"Yes. You'd have to write on them, too."

"You mean catalogue or jacket—no, they don't have jackets, do they?"

"No. Maybe I should have said you'd have to write in them, not on them."

"In them?"

"Yes. That girl out in the waiting room. Judy Cuneo. She's leaving."

Laura nodded. "To have a baby."

"Yes. And she and Jack—he works in our reproduction department—you know, Xerox and mimeograph—they may get married, too."

Laura nodded again.

"Anyhow, she not only handles the phones and reads unsols, she does RSV material for Ralph Jorgenson."

Laura looked baffled.

"Oh. Ralph is Teddy Mario and Luke Knox and Barbara Comer." He saw her bafflement grow. "Mario, Knox, Comer —they're all Ralph's pseudonyms. He writes Solus books under all those names. He's very prolific. But he can't do RSV stuff worth a damn. Or, at least, he won't try. He gets so worked up in his action scenes—whatever they are, anal, oral, straight, homo, s.m., two-way, three-way, daisy-chains—you know, all that stuff." She was looking at him in wide-eyed wonder, but he didn't seem to notice. "Anyhow, he won't write anything but action and, well, maybe he can't actually write RSV."

"*What* is RSV?"

"Oh," said Snaith, "I'm sorry. Redeeming social values. Without that, his books would be a bore. Just unrelieved screwing. Which would make them unbelievable and might

28

put them under the counter. And that sort of thing is selling less and less." He studied her for a moment. "Look. Ralph writes damn good porn. And funny porn. And it entertains lots of people who like that sort of thing. But a book has to have more than porn to have any variety and to be legitimate. So, in his case, we add it."

"But isn't that cheating?"

"Cheating? How?"

"Putting something into a book that doesn't belong there?"

"But it does belong there. There's nothing wrong with porn. The more straight honest porn, the merrier—but the reader needs a rest in between bouts of it, and the good porn authors write it in. Except Ralph. He's too single-track. We have to do it for him. But what's wrong with that? If the author wrote his own redeeming social values, would you think that was cheating?"

"N-o. I guess not."

"Well, are you against collaboration? If two people write a book, do you care who wrote which part?"

"N-o." She was deeply puzzled and unable to express her confusion, or even determine wherein it lay. "Still, a telephone operator isn't really a co-author."

"Why not? Who knows what talent lies trapped in the Bell System? Convicts have written masterpieces. Anyhow, if Ralph's books sold better, he could afford to split his royalties with someone. But he can't. He doesn't even get royalties. Just a straight sum per book. And he can't afford to split that any more than I can afford not to publish him. He helps pay the overhead. So if someone I'd have to hire anyhow can put in the social value stuff—as you said, crowd scenes, landscapes, interiors, *other* things the characters are doing or thinking about, all that sort of thing—well, then it works." He watched her for a few moments. "It's bothering you, isn't it?"

"Yes. No. I'm not sure . . ."

"Maybe you're thinking about what your mother would say."

She looked up in surprise. "No. That hadn't crossed my mind."

"Well, then?"

"Look," she said, "I'll say I want the job. But I'm seeing someone tonight I want to talk to about it. If I change my mind, may I have until tomorrow morning to tell you so?"

"Sure," said Snaith. "By all means talk to him."

Rupert put down his fork and pushed his plate away an inch or two. "I still agree with Laura." He sipped the last of his wine.

"Even to wondering if it's cheating?" challenged Jenny.

"Yes. Even to that."

"I must be missing your point," said Marc, "or at least your reasoning."

Laura looked raptly from them to Rupert, aware that the outcome of this argument would probably determine her immediate future.

"I'll try again, from a different angle," said Rupert. "You both damn well know I haven't hesitated to sponsor books that have been called pornographic. And my firm has published them. Time and again. As your firm, Marc, has every reason to know. Priam's novel is merely a recent example. But I've never sounded off in editorial meetings for any book that I didn't consider an honest work of literature. I've never knowingly supported a book that was written solely to titillate. And certainly never participated in rigging a book to sneak it within the law."

"That so?" Mark snapped. "How about *The Provocator?*"

"You call that porn?" Rupert demanded. "You call that rigged?"

"I don't call anything porn. But I sure as hell call it rigged. It was written to titillate, promoted to titillate, and made every best-seller list because it succeeded in titillating. Just because it was published by a fine old and respected house, ran nearly five hundred drooling pages and sold for nearly eight bucks doesn't make it any more or less respectable than the next *Tickling Auntie's Ass* that Linc Snaith may do as a Solus paperback at ninety-five cents or a buck and a quarter. And I wouldn't censor either of them."

"But nobody was hired to write in stuff that would get *The Provocator* past the law."

"Aren't you forgetting," asked Marc, "that when we read the original manuscript we not only advised you to circumvent the laws of libel by having the author tone down the characters of the Irish actor and the French sexpot so they wouldn't so closely resemble you-know-who, but we also urged you to have him add to the scene of the orgy at Dubrovnik. And remember what we suggested adding? A scene out of doors, contrasting the medieval, cloistered old city with the Communist-planned new city just beyond the walls. And we told you we wanted something like that added to give redeeming social value to that part of the novel."

"But the author added it himself," Rupert protested.

"What difference does that make? If Gilbert had written erotically suggestive lyrics, would you have objected to Sullivan making them politely acceptable with a beautiful score?" Marc rose and paced the dinette. "And while we're on the subject of *The Provocator*, let me remind you of something else that made us damn mad at the bluenoses. When *The Provocator* went into paperback it got banned from a lot of libraries by extralegal means, and some mass-market wholesalers wouldn't sell it—that outfit in Kentucky was one, I remember." He turned to Laura. "And if you're wondering what extralegal means are—they can be anything from some local town select-man saying to the librarian, 'Take that book off your shelves or I'll see to it that the Finance Committee cuts your budget,' to getting the fire chief to find violations in the heating system. But nobody interfered with the book in its original edition. Because the self-appointed censors think that anyone who can afford eight dollars for a book is too rich to be corrupted."

"Or maybe," suggested Rupert, "old enough not to be."

"Oh, I know that argument. It leads straight to 'Let's reduce all adult literature to a level fit for kiddies.' There are valid laws which prevent stores from selling or libraries from lend-ing a book like that to children. As if they'd read it anyhow. Look around this apartment. You've got plenty of things— from *Kama Sutra* to early Henry Miller and *The Psychology of Sex* right out in your living room and study. They were there when Anne was growing up, weren't they? Did you keep them out of her hands?"

"We did not," said Jenny. "We didn't move a volume."

"And what happened?"

Jenny shrugged. "Maybe she tried them. When she was too young, I imagine that kind of book bored her. If she was old enough to find it exciting, I imagine she got rid of her excite-ment." She looked questioningly at Laura.

Laura felt constrained to answer the look. "We didn't have books like that, but even so . . . And damn this blushing habit. I *will* get over it." She hesitated. "But mightn't books like that, even seriously intended sex books, drive people into danger-ous acts?"

"I don't know," said Jenny. "But *what* I do know is that sexuality can be stimulated in a bookless home. I grew up in one. But I was curious. And we did have a dictionary. So I looked up all the anatomical words I knew, or could overhear. For weeks I swooned over *Webster's* definition of testicles. And when I found 'penis,' well, if the nearest possible male hadn't been over seven miles from our farm, I'd never have held out until the end of my freshman year at Oberlin."

Laura glanced at Rupert. "But Damascus is a long way from Oberlin."

"True," said Jenny. "Fortunately, Dennison is just around the corner." She reflected. "Now Anne is at Wellesley. And I'm not sure what her status is. My guess is that she has experimented. And Rupert and I are not dismayed at that. He may even secretly agree with me that she should. She's got lots of sense and lots of human know-how. Quite a bit of which came from her reading. Parents aren't everything."

"Of course they're not," agreed Rupert, "but Anne was raised in a pretty decent environment. What about the environmentally underprivileged kids? In slums. In ghettos. What happens when they—" He interrupted himself and laughed ruefully. "Don't bother saying it, Marc. I know that pitifully few of them read—anything, let alone books." He looked over at Laura. "This isn't answering your question, is it? I still think the idea of writing in passages to bring an otherwise objectionable book within the law—"

"Look here," said Marc, "without for a minute accepting your 'otherwise objectionable,' let me ask you this. Suppose this horny author of Linc's—what's his name?—Ralph something . . ."

"Ralph Jorgenson," supplied Laura.

"Suppose while he was writing his book it occurred to him, either for artistic or for legal reasons, to write in some relieving nonsexual passages, and he did. That would be all right, wouldn't it? But having someone else write them in, that bugs you. Why?"

"I'm not sure," said Rupert. "But it does. I guess it's the difference between the pushover and the prostitute. The deliberateness for a crass end."

"Okay," said Marc. "Now that we've had some thousands of recorded years in which to examine the problem, what do you think society should do about the prostitute? Keep on trying to arrest and imprison her? Or recognize that the best way to get rid of such attendant evils as pimps and disease is to legalize her?"

"You know damn well I think she should be legalized. But what's that got to do with Laura's problem?" He shot a finger out at Marc. "Except that's exactly what Linc is doing. He's trying to prostitute Laura."

"The hell he is. He doesn't want her to make dirty. He wants her to make clean."

"It seems to me," said Jenny, "that you two are so screwed up arguing the moral issue and the legal issue that you've forgotten the most important one—the literary issue." She looked levelly at Laura. "Have you considered whether you can properly do the job Linc Snaith wants? Can you write well enough?"

"I don't know," said Laura. "I never thought I'd be writing parts of books." She puzzled for some moments. "How well do you have to write for *that* kind of book?"

"At least as well as Ralph Jorgensen writes clinical sex scenes," said Jenny, "and in my opinion that happens to be very well—sometimes damn near poetic."

"Ah, the sweet rhythmic climaxes," Rupert said.

"Umm," said Jenny, "I was thinking of the number of cantos, too." She turned to Marc. "I think that even without social-value additions, his books have redeeming *literary* value. Is that recognized by the courts, Marc?"

"It has been. Woolsey strongly implied it in his *Ulysses* decision. But going to court, winning, or losing and appealing— that costs more money than Linc can afford. So he wants to discourage the bluenoses by building strong legal defenses into Jorgenson's books." He turned to Laura. "And don't get the idea that if you take this job, you'll be working to thwart the law."

"No?" asked Rupert. "What else, then?"

"She'll be working to discourage the *de facto* censors.

They're the ones who thwart the law. Constantly. They make it so uncomfortable for bookstores to stock his books that they can scarcely be found anywhere except on Forty-second Street or in some other out-of-the-way shops." He swung back to Rupert. "What about Larrabee's? Their big fancy store on Madison Avenue won't carry a single Solus book. But their shop in the Village carries them all."

"That's because the Madison Avenue trade doesn't go for Solus stuff, whereas—"

"Balls!" said Marc, and Laura didn't blush. "The Madison Avenue trade goes down to the Village to buy Solus books. They don't sell them uptown because Larrabee's best customers—meaning the people who pay twenty-five dollars for every coffee-table book about flower arranging—threaten to take their trade elsewhere if Larrabee's sells porn in the high-rent district."

"I guess this isn't answering Jenny's question," said Rupert. "Can Laura write well enough to match Jorgenson's prose?"

"That's not our problem," said Marc. "Or even Laura's. I don't think she came here to find out if she might be in danger of being fired the day after she took the job. She was troubled about the—propriety of doing it." He looked questioningly at Laura.

"Yes," she said, "but now I am beginning to wonder."

"That's Linc's problem," said Marc, "and the book buyers'. If you're not good enough, they'll let you know soon enough."

"When I was leaving, Mr. Snaith said something about borrowing passages from the classics, in addition to writing in things myself. I'm not sure I know what he meant."

Rupert chuckled. "It's an interesting idea. If the hero is expressing himself too graphically, I suppose he could quote The Song of Solomon instead. Would that work, Marc? Or maybe break up a hot chapter on shipboard by having the girl remember a scenic passage from *Moby Dick*."

"Or from anyone's," mused Jenny.

"As a matter of fact," said Marc, "it wouldn't always work.

There have been several attempts in this century—true, mostly in small Bible Belt towns—to have The Song of Solomon, the story of Lot and his daughters and several other 'went in unto' scenes banned from Old Testaments used in Sunday schools. One was actually printed, but it cost so much to do a special edition for a limited market that it was economically impractical."

"In all fairness to Laura," said Rupert, "I think she should know that she's being asked to do something no other publisher has ever suggested—at least to my knowledge."

"And that," said Jenny, "doesn't seem to me to be the issue, either. If it's wrong, it wouldn't matter how often it had been done before. And if it's right, what harm if it's also unprecedented?"

"I guess," said Laura, "it's finally up to me. I really am grateful for . . ." Her voice trailed off as the phone rang. Rupert crossed into the study and spoke for a few minutes.

Jenny rose and carried the dessert plates into the kitchen while Marc turned to Laura. "Later . . . let's talk some more about this."

She nodded.

Rupert came back into the room as Jenny emerged from the kitchen.

"That was Moira. Priam's been arrested."

9

The Community Room in the basement of the Morningside Presbyterian Church was better known to most New Yorkers than the church itself. At least, it appeared in the papers more often. In the church proper the Reverend Samuel Toomey paid nominal respect to his creed's Calvinist origin. In the Community Room he had increasingly, during his twenty-odd years' tenure, expressed his enthusiasm for the new and controversial. He had championed civil rights in the fifties before Harlem crept westward to where his church stood at 111th Street near Broadway. He had welcomed protests against our involvement in Vietnam when only our advisers were involved. He had championed Women's Liberation when Ms. was still a manuscript. As a consequence, his congregation and his Community Room became increasingly well attended by neighborhood blacks and by Columbia and Barnard students. Among his most popular downstairs attractions were amateur productions of experimental plays ("After all," he'd explain, "my church is *off* Broadway") and readings by the more free-wheeling, less inhibited writers. An hour before Moira phoned Rupert, Priam had concluded reading a group of his poems to a mostly young audience and commenced the recital of what might be called the confrontation scene from *Consenting in Private*.

He was nearing the middle of that dialogue-in-utero when a balding young man rose from the audience.

"I demand you stop reading that pornography!"

Priam paused. Several voices from the audience yelled

"Shut up!"; "Sit down!"; "Let him read!" Reverend Toomey, who had been sitting onstage behind Priam, stood and made quieting motions. Priam cleared his throat and went on reading.

The man moved out into the aisle. "In the name of decency, stop!"

A couple of men behind the interrupter rose and started toward him. Priam raised his arms. "If the gentleman has something to say, I'll yield this platform to him as soon as I've finished."

"You're not going to finish!" the man shouted and came purposefully down the aisle. The two other men were joined by a buxom woman, and the three of them grabbed the protester. In the rear of the little auditorium, an elderly man went quickly to a pay phone in the lobby.

"Please," Reverend Toomey called out, "no violence!" He murmured something to Priam, who nodded. "If the gentleman wants to explain his objection, he may do so from the floor or wait until Mr. Wendell is finished and then come to the podium. In any event, please unhand him."

The balding youth was reluctantly released. He pointed at Priam. "What you are reading is perverted. It describes an unnatural act between an unborn brother and sister."

Priam replied calmly, "I *thought* you'd misunderstood. The participating embryos happen to be unborn brothers."

The protesting young man leaped past the threesome who had restrained him and jumped up the short steps to the stage. He shouted to the audience. "You see! Not content with portraying incest, he's made it homosexual incest. It would be impossible to go farther." He swung toward Priam, who, advancing, was struck by the tall man's flailing arm, which Priam grabbed, spinning the man backward toward Toomey's vacated chair. Priam, again at the podium, loudly declared, "Impossible to go farther? The hell it would! In the next edition it will also be miscegenation—one twin will be black and the other one white."

The audience delightedly applauded this announcement.

"And here," said Reverend Toomey, "I believe they come now."

Two radio-car policemen were striding down the aisle, and indeed—one was black, the other white.

10

The desk sergeant at the 26th Precinct on West 126th Street looked pained. He turned away from Priam and the tall young man, who had identified himself as Francis Wills, and said to Marc, "But if I let them go, how do I know they won't disturb the peace again?"

"Sergeant, it's perfectly clear that only this man"—Marc pointed to Wills—"caused a disturbance. My client was reading to an audience. This man interrupted and stormed the stage."

"And got spun into a chair by him," charged Wills.

"Because he swung at me," said Priam.

"Sergeant, I believe this man"—Reverend Toomey pointed at Wills—"created a disturbance in my church last year."

"Yeah?"

"I'm quite sure it was he. We were having a performance of *No Exit*. He was among several who tried to stop it."

"The actors were naked," exclaimed Wills.

"It's by Sartre," explained Toomey. He addressed Wills. "You seem to consider yourself some kind of Watch and Ward Society."

"I happen to be vice-president of Youth for Decency," said Wills with dignity.

"I thought I'd seen him before," Laura blurted. "He spoke at Indianapolis a couple of years ago. It was an A.C.E. convention."

"Did you say AC-DC?" asked the sergeant suspiciously.

"A.C.E. Americans for Clean Entertainment."

The sergeant pondered. "Youth for Decency. Americans for Clean Entertainment. Sound like a couple of grand organizations."

"They're both completely shitty," announced Moira.

"Lady," said the sergeant, "if you didn't have a beautiful brogue, I'd book you for saying that." He turned again to the antagonists. "Do either of you want to bring charges?"

Priam waved the idea away.

"I do. Against him," said Wills, pointing at Toomey. "For presenting indecent performances."

The sergeant turned to the arresting officers. "Did you see anything indecent?"

"When we got there," said the black, "nothing was happening, except they'd been sort of fighting. Least that's what someone said."

"So what was indecent?"

Wills nodded toward Priam. "That book he's holding. He was reading it. Out loud. And there were ladies present."

The sergeant asked Marc, "Mind if I see your client's book?"

Marc glanced at Rupert, who said, "By all means."

"What about it, Priam?" asked Marc. "Unless you're willing, they'd have to make formal charges and obtain a warrant to seize the book."

Priam took the volume from his pocket. "Another reader's another reader." He handed it up to the sergeant, who examined the jacket with seeming disappointment at its plainness, opened it and started to read. After a few moments he flipped to another page and read some more. "Does this stuff mean anything?"

Priam opened his mouth but Marc restrained him.

"I'll tell you what it means," said Wills. "May I come up and whisper it to you?"

The sergeant looked inquiringly at Marc, who shook his head. "I think not, Sergeant. We'd have to know what he was claiming. Let him say it out loud."

"Not in front of these ladies." Wills indicated Laura and Jenny. "Or that woman." He pointed toward Moira.

"Sergeant," said Marc, "perhaps I can help out Mr. Wills." He turned to him. "Are you trying to inform the sergeant that within that book are several pages describing incestuous homosexuality?"

"And miscegenation!" added Wills.

"Not in that edition," countered Marc. He turned back to the sergeant. "I believe you will find that even if the act described had been performed onstage, a charge of indecency could be countered by the social value of the total content as well as by claims of simulation and artistic license. Certainly, reading about it is permissible anywhere. I might add that the acts have often been portrayed in the art of many ancient religions, and that the participants in the book you are holding, while not adult, are certainly consenting."

Hours later on that July night Laura was still awake—and alone. The fact that she needn't have been alone was the chief contribution to her wakefulness.

Marc had wanted her to come back to his apartment from the 26th Precinct. Instinctively, she knew that to go there at that moment would be a commitment which, physically, she wanted to make. But she also knew that, emotionally, she was deeply torn between her swift response to Marc—it was less than a week since she'd met him—and fear of what she didn't even know enough to call postcoital guilt.

Over sandwiches and coffee with him in the all-night diner around the corner from her hotel, she was still warmed by the recollection that when Marc had kissed her in the cab, he'd held her sweatered breast. She was also annoyed by the knowledge that he'd been only the second man to do so, and that the other had been a forgettable Damascene who'd taken her to a few drive-in movies. In those same drive-ins, she'd glimpsed classmates in far more complicated embraces, and other girls whom she couldn't identify as classmates because only an occasional foot and leg were visible against, or sticking out of, a dark car window.

As her reading had informed her of what was going on among the suns and planets of the galaxy and the pulsars and quasars beyond it, so her observation and the conversation of her friends had made her aware of what was transpiring in her town, and far more intensely in the worlds outside. She accepted the fact of the activity without personal realization of it.

Nor did she know how patiently Marc was prepared to go along with her reluctance. She knew that he'd been born in Philadelphia, educated in Cambridge and worked in New York. She didn't know how this geographical limitation contributed to a general assumption that the rest of America was backward. Marc would have expected to make far faster progress with a girl from the Northeast, or perhaps from certain large cities which had managed astonishing degrees of sophistication despite the handicap of a West Coast, mid-continent or even Southern locale. But from a Middle Western small town! Had she known of Marc's ignorance of mid-American life-style progress, she still wouldn't have realized how long a warm-up he was prepared for. When he alluded, between sips of coffee, to the swift changes she'd so recently experienced—New York, a lonely hotel room, new acquaintances unlike any she'd had before, a decidedly odd-ball job offer—he was assuring her, more subtly than she had the experience to understand, that he wouldn't rush her. What *he* didn't know was the degree of commitment implicit in his patience.

Now, sleepless, Laura pushed aside her thoughts of Marc, his apartment, the taxi ride. She had to give an answer to Lincoln Snaith, Jr. Tomorrow. If she took the job, what would her mother say? If she didn't take the job, could she hope to find another before her money ran out? And if her money ran out, she'd have to go back to Ludgrove—and to Mother. Which, she was sure, meant something defeating and disastrous. It wasn't that she disliked her mother. Indeed, in a traditional sense, she loved her. Jessica Conroy was a forbidding woman who could nevertheless be warmly affectionate to the things that were hers: her handsome house, her firm place in Ludgrove's society and her growing place in America's, her loyal adherents within the national chapters of A.C.E., her daughter and, on all public and many family occasions, her meekly providing husband.

Until the other night on the phone, Laura had never argued with her mother. She'd pleaded with her, nagged at her until she'd won permission and funds for this timid trial in New York. But they'd gotten along well enough, because Laura never betrayed her mother's concept of filial loyalty. It would be so easy, so comfortable in a sense, to refuse Snaith's offer, to fail in other job attempts, to go home, to do polite and proper good works, to marry some boy next door, to live with him in the same best part of Ludgrove she'd always known . . .

Laura pushed herself nervously out of bed, paced the little room, then stood at the window looking down into the small fragment of Lexington Avenue visible below. Even now, at nearly three o'clock, there was, to her, a surprising degree of activity. A taxi came to a double-parking halt to discharge a man and woman. The man was in a dinner jacket, the woman stood unsteadily in a ground-sweeping gown. Behind it, another cab and a newspaper truck honked angrily, then guiltily stopped their honking for a moment while a police car, its red roof light whirling, sirened up and swept past. The lights at Sixty-third switched from red to green, and presently back to red again. A couple, arms around each other's waists, walked southward, stopped, and pressing tightly against each other, kissed long and passionately. Laura watched them until they broke their embrace and walked on more hurriedly.

She turned back toward her bed. She'd call Snaith in the morning and she knew what she must say to him.

This time she fell asleep.

Dear Mother:

I've found a job. Actually, I've been working at it since Monday. Tabard Press is a new publishing house, although they've already done some very worthwhile things. Professor Forman's study of Emily Dickinson's family didn't sell a great many, but it's beginning to be used in college courses. And they almost won a National Book Award in *belles lettres* for *After Transcendentalism*, the essays by Margaret Fuller's great-grandniece. I'm working at the switchboard, doing clerical odds and ends and occasionally I'm allowed to do a little writing in connection with some of their books. I'm learning a lot about publishing and even think I've broadened my vocabulary.

Mr. Snaith, the owner, is a very nice man who seems to take a lot of interest in my progress. He reviews and edits everything I write—he even shows some of it to a young friend of his who also happens to be his lawyer. I've met Rupert Hayes of William Simmons & Sons—remember, years ago you gave me their edition of Hawthorne's *Twice-Told Tales*. Rupert and Jenny—they insisted that I call them that—have had me to their home twice. One time it was to that party where Nadia Norse saw me. The other time was last week when they gave a small dinner. My escort was Rupert's lawyer. You'd like him.

Anyhow, I'm now earning enough to manage on my own, especially when I find a less expensive, proper place to share with a roommate. Love to you and Daddy.

Laura

13

"Marc."

"Laura. Hi."

"I hate to bother you at the office. But just before I left for work this morning, Mother phoned."

"Yes?"

"So I can't see you tonight. She's coming to New York. Wants me to meet her for dinner. Marc, she's awfully angry."

"Why? What's up?"

"I'd written her about my job. And I had to say it was Tabard Press. I didn't tell her exactly everything I was doing.

But she knows they publish Solus Books. She's going to try to make me leave there."

"Just how can she do that?"

"I know. She can't really. I mean I won't. But it's going to be awful."

"I'd like to rally round."

"No! That would only make it worse. I mean, she'd be sure to remember you from the time you had her on the witness stand."

"So? Now she can find out what a gentle soul I am on other occasions."

"Marc, I just know I have to face her alone."

"Maybe I can join you later. For coffee or something."

"But if the two of you fought . . . I mean, I couldn't stand it. I mean—"

"I hope I know what you mean. And on the off chance I'm right, I'd better get together with her sooner or later. Look. Don't get so up-tight about it. Relax. Maybe after dinner we can take her to an X-rated movie."

Laura managed a giggle. "Maybe you'd better take me to one first. I've never been. Oh, Marc. I so dread this evening."

Jessica Carrol Conroy was a small woman, demure, slim, gray-blond and prettily featured. She could, and often did, produce a winning smile. She couldn't, and never tried to, suppress entirely the steel in her eyes. Those who, on first meeting her, looked down from their superior height and dismissed the rumors of her imperious force, had forgotten Napoleon, Victoria and the pocket battleship.

When she made one of her infrequent visits to New York, Jessica always stayed at the Comstock, a small and very proper residential hotel in the West Fifties. Jessica didn't know whether it was named for the founder of the Society for the Suppression of Vice, or one of the Comstocks in Nebraska, Michigan, upper New York, Minnesota, Wisconsin or Texas, or just for the famous Lode, but any of these images suited her devotion to vice suppression, small-town America and wealth. Suited her, as did the half-veiled little chapeaux one of which —whether at a Ludgrove social, on an A.C.E. dias or, as now in her hotel room and prepared to descend to the Comstock's no-nonsense dining room—she always wore. When she let Laura in, she had permitted her cheek to be kissed, had coolly replied that she was well and that Daddy was likewise, and seating herself on a petit-point armchair, had instantly given it the appearance of a throne. Laura had sunk down at one end of a small sofa and grown in nervousness as her mother silently regarded her. Finally Jessica spoke.

"Why did you do it?"

"Take a job? That's why I came to New York."

"But why *there*? Out of all the publishers in this city?"

"I was lucky to get it. There aren't many jobs for inexperienced girls in publishing. They want secretarial skills."

"But you wanted to do editorial work. Or so you pretended."

"And I am—I will. Mr. Snaith has promised me."

"I presume you're familiar with the kind of things he publishes."

"Of course I am. I wrote you about some of them."

"And very craftily failed to mention his Solus books."

"But that's only a small part—"

"I'm quite sure you've been reading them."

"I've seen them." Then Laura's voice took on a hint of defiance. "Yes. I've read one or two."

"And what did you think of them?"

"I was shocked." She rushed on before Jessica could interrupt. "I was shocked that I knew so little. About what they described."

"Do you think it necessary to know more than you did?"

"Yes. Sex is part of the world—of living. And it's a part that I—that everyone needs to know."

"No decent girl, or man, needs to know about unnatural things."

"But maybe they aren't unnatural. Just different."

"I'm afraid that what you truly mean is 'just degrading.' "

"Mother. I'm old enough to be grown-up, even if I'm not really. Not yet. But I think I know that any kind of relationship can be natural or degrading, and it has nothing to do with what people are doing. It depends on the people doing it. How they feel about it—and each other."

"Do you know what sadists do? Or homosexuals?"

"Yes. Some."

"And I suppose you approve."

"I don't think it's up to me to approve or not. It's up to them."

"But suppose everybody did that!"

"Then the world would be very dull—for people who don't like to hurt each other. Or prefer the opposite sex." She rose and walked to a window. She stared across rooftops for a moment. Then she turned and put her hands behind her on the sill. "Mother. Being here, meeting people—yes, even reading those books—I've learned that there are more kinds of personalities than I'd guessed. And that people can be different at different times. That sounds simple to me now. But I had to find it out. Do you know what I mean?"

"I'm afraid so." Jessica sighed heavily. "You studied literature. I thought you had learned the difference between great books and—and trash."

"I've found out that I didn't study literature. I thought I was reading *The Canterbury Tales*, for instance. But now I know that what I studied was a—a deodorized version of it. Whole sections had been left out of the edition we read at school."

"And properly so."

"I don't believe it. In college, they're old enough to read everything Chaucer wrote."

"No matter how vulgar?"

"No matter how true—how honest to the life and times of his era."

"Indeed? Then why don't you eat with your fingers? He did. Why don't you go for weeks without bathing? He did. I'm sure you can find books that will tell you what perfumes he used to cover his stench. Why don't you use outdoor trenches or openings in turret flooring for a bathroom?"

"But I'm not talking about doing everything he did. Or everything he wrote about. I'm talking about reading what he had to say, every act he felt it necessary to his art to describe. Or should Botticelli have covered Venus' breasts opaquely?"

Jessica retreated for a moment into a cold contempt. When she spoke it was with the tone of a sly inquisitor. "Just how did you suddenly find out that you hadn't read the whole book?"

"I've told you. I've met people here. Intelligent people and—"

"Ah, of course! Like that Priam Wendell that Nadia Norse saw you with."

"And others. Look, Mother. Let's not fight. I haven't seen you for a while. Let's have dinner and talk about something else."

"Yes. We'll have dinner. But I don't think you realize how deeply you're offending me. I came here because I have no intention of standing by idly and watching you pursue this kind of life. I mean it, Laura. You're to come home."

Laura shook her head slowly. "I don't want to offend you. But I don't want to go home, either."

"Suppose your father and I ordered you to?"

"I hope you won't, because that would make everything very unpleasant. I'm going to stay here, Mother."

Jessica considered her next words carefully. "I suppose you feel some kind of friendliness or loyalty to this Snaith person."

"I'm working for him. Shouldn't I be loyal?"

"I think so. And for that reason, I suggest you quit his firm at once and come back to Ludgrove."

Laura looked at her uncomprehendingly.

"Americans for Clean Entertainment has grown," Jessica went on quietly. "It's bigger and more powerful than you imagine. New members. More contributions. We have many targets to attack. So many that we have to choose which to aim at next. You'd be surprised how very persuasive we can be with bookstores and libraries, even when they fight back. We can bring more local suits than most publishers, particularly smaller ones, have money to defend against."

"Just to make me come home! I'd never leave here, then."

"Not just to make you come home. Our purpose, of course, is to stop the publishing of pornography." Jessica rose. "Now, let's have dinner."

Laura pushed herself away from the window sill. She might have been on the point of running out. Then she seemed to gather herself. "May I use your phone? I broke an engagement to have dinner with you. I'd like someone to pick me up here after. Maybe you should meet him."

"Him? Is this your source of information about what isn't vulgar any more?"

Laura, crossing to the phone, didn't answer.

15

The dining room of the Hotel Comstock didn't inspire conversation. The décor was starkly ordinary. The food, if not unmentionable, certainly wasn't worth talking about. The diners were pallid and seemed imminently prepared to fade back into the woodwork.

Laura and Jessica proceeded almost wordlessly through a characterless consommé to a London broil which seemed to have been flavored in the Thames, and finally to a weary rice pudding. Once Laura, trying to tamp down her smoldering anger at her mother's threat, had been on the point of making some advance comment about Marc, but decided that anything she might say would probably worsen what she was sure would be an unpleasant scene. When he appeared in the dining-room entrance, she made a worried, tentative gesture and he crossed to them. Laura couldn't remember ever seeing him before in so dark a suit or with so somber a tie on his white shirt. Evidently he had prepared to Make a Good Impression.

Jessica, noticing his approach, gave him the benefit of a studied indifference.

"Mother, this is a friend of mine. Marc Holland."

"How do you do, Mrs. Conroy?"

Jessica suddenly recognized him. "Mr. Holland and I have met."

"I'm glad to see you again—" Marc began.

"—Under equally uncomfortable circumstances," concluded Jessica.

"I was hoping," said Marc, "that neither of us would feel that we were here as adversaries." He remained standing politely beside an empty chair.

"Sit down, Marc," said Laura.

Her mother raised her eyebrows at her. "I'm more accustomed to Mr. Holland standing up—and browbeating me."

Marc sat. "I'm not in a browbeating mood. I was defending a client that day. I'm not defending anything now."

"Perhaps you should be," said Jessica coldly. And when Marc looked puzzled, she went on, "Don't you at least feel defensive about having placed Laura, and me, in a shocking situation?"

"Mother! Marc merely introduced me to a man who had a job opening."

"Of course—and with the full knowledge that the man is a publisher of pornography." She looked bitterly at Marc. "I suppose it didn't occur to you that by insinuating Laura into that atmosphere you were making a mockery of me."

"I think you are exaggerating the atmosphere of Tabard Press."

"I could scarcely exaggerate the nature of Solus books. I doubt that anyone could work there without being contaminated by them. Even though Laura, of course, wouldn't have anything to do with such filth."

"Mrs. Conroy. Have you ever read a Solus book?"

"Certainly not! I've been shown excerpts—they were more than enough for my stomach."

"If you read one in its entirety, you might find it amusing. Possibly even"—Marc hesitated—"even pleasantly captivating."

"Don't you mean titillating?"

Marc sighed. "Yes. I honestly do. Titillation isn't bad. It's a normal response to many artistic forms. Some of the greatest painters have employed it."

"Mr. Holland. I'm not going to permit you to twist my acceptance of—of a Rubens into approval of a dirty postcard."

"I quite agree with your unwillingness. I don't like dirty postcards either."

"Really? You astonish me. I gathered from your remarks in court that day that you didn't draw the line at anything."

Marc leaned forward intently. "Then you misunderstood me. I draw the line of my personal preferences at many points. But I don't know how— I don't believe there is a satisfactory way for the law to draw a line." He moved his chair closer to the table. "The dirty postcard may show parts of the body or bodily acts that we'd rather not see portrayed in that context. But the same parts and the same acts might be portrayed, and have been portrayed, by great sculptors, painters, dancers—all with consummate art. The problem is that no matter how you try to phrase a law intended to ban the postcard and permit the art, you get into areas of human judgment. Of opinions about what is merely crass and what is essentially beautiful. What was the intent of the creator of the postcard, the creator of the statue?"

"I maintain that Solus books are created solely for money."

"So are automobiles."

"Nonsense. Automobiles are a necessity. A means of transport."

"So are Solus books."

"Mr. Holland! I know you have no respect for me. Perhaps you could try to have some for my daughter."

"But, Mother, I think what Marc said is true. Also a bit funny."

"Funny? At my expense?" Jessica rose. "If you will excuse me." To Laura she said, "I will expect to hear from you presently. This evening. And not too late." She moved briskly out of the room.

They sat for a silent minute. "I guess I messed that up. And all I was trying to do was to get to know your mother."

"Mother isn't going to change, Marc. And I don't want you to."

"Which leaves things worse than they were before."

"Yes. And even worse than you think they are. She's telling me to come home or else."

"Or else what?"

"She'll—that is, A.C.E. will try to put Tabard Press out of business. Start so many local suits against their books that they'll run out of money trying to defend them. Can they do that, Marc?"

Marc laughed hollowly. "I think one suit might do it."

"Mother. You asked me to call you."

"Where are you?"

A pause. "In Marc Holland's bedroom."

"What—why?"

"Because that's where his phone is."

"And where is *he?*"

"In the living room where I left him."

"And you're accustomed to going into strange men's bedrooms?"

"No, I'm not. But maybe it's time I got a little used to it. And, Mother, Marc isn't a strange man."

"I find him very strange."

"That's because he's different. You must agree he's intelligent."

"I think he's clever. Machiavellian. Is he Jewish?"

"I don't know. Was Machiavelli?"

"You're obviously interested in this man but you don't even know his religion. Holland? Holland? Of course you can't tell by names any more, but there *were* a lot of Dutch Jews."

"Holland isn't a Dutch name. It's a Dutch place."

"Stop quibbling."

"Anyhow, Mother, you can't deny that Marc's good-looking."

"His type scarcely appeals to me."

"All right. You asked me to call you. Here I am."

"I merely want to make it quite clear that you are to leave that job. To leave New York—to come home."

"And you know that I don't intend to."

"Then blame yourself for any consequences."

After she replaced the receiver, Laura remained sitting on the bed. Strangely, she didn't feel upset. Or even worried. Just, maybe, a little older. And, at twenty-two, that's not a bad feeling.

. . . *and, collapsing in shuddering gasps, she rolled reluctantly from his body. Phil rested an indebted hand on her cheek, permitted it to stray to her other one, and fell asleep.*

Laura turned the page of typescript to the next chapter.

On the adjoining bed, Neill and Patrick were still at it.

Laura put down the page. This was clearly a spot where something should be interlarded. Something to relieve the tension, quite apart from injecting social value. She reflected. The scene was a motel bedroom. The time, midmorning, probably about eleven. The season was autumn. The people—the girl and Patrick—had encountered Neill and Phil in the cocktail bar the previous evening. Now it was about twelve hours and uncountable variations and arrangements later. Something *must* have been going on outside this room. "Write about things you know," her teacher in Eng. Comp 101 had insisted. Well, then. Suppose, when the girl and Patrick drove into town the night before, they'd passed a campus with some kind of pre-game activity going on. She could go back twenty pages and write that in—describing the college buildings and the group-nature of the students. Now outside in the late morning's fall sunlight, a band could go by, some students trailing behind it. She could suggest that they were torn between stirred enthusiasm and chagrin at seeming to participate in long-outmoded ceremony. Would they be on their way to the stadium? No, too early. To a pre-game rally? That was better. Only, it sounded too much like Damascus and she knew by now that Damascus wasn't typical of the seventies college scene. Nevertheless, practically all schools still played football, and there *were* bands and cheerleaders. Maybe, when the students were going by outside, she could have a couple of them notice the blinds down in the motel windows and make appreciative comments . . . She fed some paper into her typewriter and sat with fingers suspended over the keys. The switchboard buzzed and she flipped a key. "Yes, Mr. Sn— Lincoln?"

"Laura. I'm sending Jack out to watch the board. I'd like you to come in here for a minute."

"Certainly." Jack, reproduction machinist and boyfriend of the now-departed Judy Cuneo, ambled out.

"How's Judy—and the baby?"

"Back home. Don't rush." He folded himself into Laura's chair. "I'd rather do this than run those mimeos."

As soon as she entered Snaith's office, Laura saw the worry on his face. He waved her to a chair and paced behind his desk.

"Laura, has anyone been asking you what you do here?"

"Asked? I've told a few people. Mark and Rupert and Jenny Hayes—and Mother."

"What did you tell your mother?"

"Just that I ran the board, did clerical work. And some writing. I didn't tell her what kind. It would have upset her." She seemed to remember something. "Oh . . . and some of the girls at the Barbizon. But I didn't tell them more than I told Mother. There was one new girl there. At breakfast in a drugstore a couple of days ago, she sat next to me. She wanted to know what kind of writing, and she mentioned Solus books."

"What did you say?"

"I don't remember exactly. Something vague about doing editorial work on one of them."

"Did she want to know more?"

"I think so. But I didn't tell her. Why?"

"Jack was just in here. There's a man he's encountered a few times in the elevator, for several days now. He's asked Jack questions about Judy Cuneo. Jack came and told me because he couldn't figure any sensible reason for the questions unless the man is spying on us. What about the new girl at the Barbizon?"

"Janet? I've forgotten her last name. She's older than I am. She says she wants to get into publishing too. That's why she was asking me."

"Where's she from?"

"I'm not sure. I don't remember whether she even mentioned her college—if she went to one. I could try to find out."

"Better not. And don't tell her any more. Not until I can talk to Marc."

"But suppose she were to know exactly what I'm doing. It's not a crime."

"No. But it might be made to sound bad. Let's just watch ourselves." He turned his back on her and faced the window. "If someone were spying on us, have you any idea who it might be?"

She answered too quickly. "No. Of course not." Then she added more naturally, "Someone who wants to make trouble, obviously. When are you seeing Marc?"

"At lunch. Why?"

"I just wondered."

She went back to the reception desk. After a few moments, she put through a call.

"Marc, Lincoln told me you're lunching today. And what it's about. Has he told you yet?"

"Yes."

"Well. It's okay to tell him everything I told you. If you think it has any connection."

"Thanks, Laura. I was going to ask you about that."

18

The smallest and least known of New Jersey's counties is Guernsey, a sliver set among Union, Morris, Essex and Somerset. Mansfield, Guernsey's county seat, is five miles north of Plainfield and eight miles southeast of Morristown. Its twenty thousand inhabitants are a mixture of middle-class New York commuters and an increasing proportion of blue-collar workers in its textile industry. In the northwest part of town are the larger houses—many of them with acreage—the more expensive shops, the high school and the Mansfield Public Library. In 1940 Hester Morehouse had come there as an assistant librarian. Nowadays she was chief librarian and known in Mansfield's various social strata as friend of the students, good companion in literature, prickly nettle in every local controversy and—to the unregenerate elders, to the self-satisfied ignorant and the dogged preservers of the status quo —as a meddling pain in the ass.

Her considerable number of library-card holders was her pride. But that majority of Mansfield's citizens who never entered the library was her despair. Over the years she had attempted many devices to lure non-book-readers through her doors. All had failed. In 1971, about a year before Laura Conroy came to New York, Hester had made another brave attempt. She had established an "Invitation to Reading" section: a group of shelves which she stocked with light, funny, diverting novels plus more how-to-garden, how-to-diet, how-to-travel books than she'd ever displayed before. Then, remembering that she'd won occasional flurries of new readers over the years for books ranging in time and off-book-page notoriety from *Hecate County* to *Portnoy's Complaint* (which had also produced mild protests and threatened-but-never-consummated legal actions), she put in some carefully selected mild erotica. Among these was *Ecstatic Excursions,* an omnibus Tabard Press volume of three once-notorious novels no longer either sensational or in copyright (Cabell's *Jurgen,* Bodenheim's *Replenishing Jessica* and Louy's *Aphrodite*) plus one novel which Tabard had published two years before as a Solus Book —*Miss Baker's Dozen* by Teddy Mario, who was, of course, Ralph Jorgenson cum grace notes by Judy Cuneo.

In the ensuing year, the Invitation to Reading section did, indeed, produce a few new library users. And the erotica in its midst evoked the expected grumbles, plaints and threats. All of which came to nothing. Until late summer 1972, six weeks after Laura Conroy arrived in New York.

The temporary injunction which suddenly removed *Ecstatic Excursions* from Hester Morehouse's shelves produced a small sensation in Mansfield. Which wasn't surprising in a town of its size.

Its effects in New York were more limited.

"Why," asked Judy Cuneo over the phone to Lincoln Snaith, "have I been subpoenaed as a witness? How can I go down there? Who do I leave the baby with?"

"What the hell did they put it in the library for?" asked Ralph Jorgenson. "I don't write library books."

"There's no question," said Marc to Snaith. "We've checked out the complaints. They're local A.C.E. members."

"Of course it's Mother's doing," said Laura, "it's part of what she threatened."

"I know," said Marc, "but that's not your fault."

"Funny that she didn't wait to attack a book *I'd* worked on, instead of Judy's."

"She wouldn't have done that. Putting you on the stand would have connected her name with the wrong side of the case."

Laura thought about that. "You know, Marc. For a minute it almost sounded tempting."

19

Hester Morehouse was far from unprepared to appear in court. In a lifetime of espousing often unpopular causes, in a librarianship during which she had, time and again, circulated and defended books to the dismay of one or another segment of her community, she had often contemplated the possibility that some day she might end up before the bench. When the summons to show cause why the temporary restraining order on *Ecstatic Excursions* should not be made permanent finally arrived on a morning in August, her lawyer had long ago been selected.

Jay Meeker from Morristown had served three fiery terms in the State Legislature, had twice run for Congress, both times unsuccessfully because he refused to temper his views on abortion reform, busing to achieve racial balance and his philosophical opposition to both national parties over the Eisenhower-Kennedy-Johnson-Nixon Vietnam policy. He was a widower and Hester had never married. The extent of their relationship had aroused speculation—about which neither of them gave a damn. They were not merely consenting adults who cherished their privacy, they were also in their fifties and felt entitled to prerogatives currently being taken by, and often extended to, teen-agers.

Jay Meeker had frequently represented the Civil Liberties Union in Jersey cases. When Hester was summoned she called Jay. And the N.J.C.L.U., appointing him to present their amicus-curiae brief, took over the costs of the defense.

Lincoln Snaith, Jr., rallying to his book's cause, and Judy

Cuneo, his former employee, both having been subpoenaed as unwilling witnesses for the prosecution, Marc Holland naturally was requested to sit in with Jay as an associate, who, from out of state, could plead only at the pleasure of the court.

On the second Saturday in August, Hester had requested the Library Board—of which she was, of course, not a member —to meet with her. Jay knew its members well, but thought it advisable for Marc to attend. So Marc rented a car, picked up Laura, and at a few minutes to one, walked into the Mansfield library.

On the way down they had been discussing Laura's living arrangements. She was still at the Barbizon. She was still, in theory, looking for a less expensive place. Marc was suggesting that cohabitation was not only economical but also a great little old way of getting to know each other. Laura wasn't saying no. Nor was she yet saying yes. Indeed, on this subject she was saying very little. Certainly not that two weeks before, she had visited Jenny Hayes's doctor—Jenny having been pledged to silence—and obtained a prescription for the Pill. Marc, knowing nothing of this, was continuing his policy of prodding on occasion and patience at all times.

Meanwhile, he'd noticed a subtle change in Laura. A greater self-assuredness or, at least, less naïveté. Without having altered her appearance, other than to discard the ribbon that had tied back her ash-blond hair so that now it fell straight down around her shoulders, her aspect had matured. Her gaze, still essentially innocent, had become frank and often searching. She seemed less compelled to fill a momentary silence with words, and when she spoke it was sometimes with bantering ease. He put the change down to a variety of causes. First of all, an intelligent girl, she'd rapidly begun to adjust to a world vastly larger than she'd known before. More important, he attributed the development to the new friends she'd met— especially, he was happy to admit, himself. And then, there was the break with her mother. Any girl raised as she had been might have bounced backward from this rupture, but Laura, like a tennis ball free of undercut, seemed to have bounded forward. It wasn't, he was sure, merely the physical separation from home, but much more the deliberate refusal any longer to accept maternal dominance.

Marc was correct in all these surmises. However, he knew nothing of a little incident which, possibly more than any other experience, had influenced her rather swift growing up. It had occurred in the preceding month. She'd had a lunch date with Sylvia, Rupert Hayes's secretary, and was waiting in her antechamber office while—she could see them through the open door—Sylvia sat beside Rupert's desk and Priam Wendell lounged on a couch opposite. Rupert was dictating to Sylvia and looking up frequently with questioning glances at Priam. Each time, Priam nodded agreement to whatever had been dictated and Rupert continued. When they finished, Sylvia came to the door with Priam and Rupert following her. Rupert, greeting Laura, had asked her how the job was going while Sylvia went to her suddenly buzzing phone and glanced up to tell Rupert that Boston was returning his call. Rupert, excusing himself, closed his door. That was when Priam had asked Laura if she'd lunched yet, adding some interest of his own in her new job. Laura started to say that she and Sylvia —when Sylvia broke in that now she'd such a load of typing that if she wasn't leaving Laura on her own, she'd really better work right through a sandwich lunch at her desk. And Laura suddenly found herself out in the elevator corridor with Priam, protesting that she didn't have time for anything so elaborate, and doubtless fattening, as the nearby restaurant whose Gallic syllables he'd mentioned. Out on Park Avenue, Priam took her arm firmly, assured her that the maître d' was a pal who'd whisk them out as early as she wished, and glancing appreciatively at Laura's figure, smiled away her fear of calories.

Over lunch, an elegantly prepared bit of Sole Véronique— the grapes, Priam assured her, were the best part—and a bottle of wine, he asked her about her job and drew her out on the techniques of interrupting sex scenes with less intense and less erotic material. She found herself talking easily about her contributions to a Jorgenson opus and casually accepting his apparently ingenuous inquiries about how much she read of Jorgenson's material. She didn't realize that he'd asked her another question when, sipping again at her wine, she asked him if it came from the same part of France where he and Moira lived.

He sat back for a moment and eyed her with amusement. "You did that well," he said and she was about to ask him what he meant when he said no, it was a Poligny-Montrachet and came from Burgundy, adding—to her inquiring look—that Burgundy was another part of France. And she said she knew *that* but she'd always thought that Burgundy was red like the color of a dress and he explained that it could be white, too, and suddenly said, "You're unique," and she asked why. "Because you aren't afraid to admit that you don't know something." And she responded that she wasn't afraid to admit that she hadn't the faintest idea what he'd meant before when he said that she'd done something well.

"Didn't you hear my question?" he asked, and she shook her head. "I asked you whether Jorgenson's writing affected you physically, turned you on. And I thought you knew the question was preliminary to a pass and that you were brushing me off adroitly with a question about the wine."

She looked at him gravely for as long as it took her to put this all together, and then she said, "But why should you make a pass? Aren't you and Moira . . .?"

"Yes," he said, "we are. But we also sometimes do. Separately."

Laura thought that over. "But what made you think that we—"

"I *didn't*. I didn't *know*. I was searching out your mood. If you'd been so inclined, we might have enjoyed—oh, for Christ's sake! Don't make me talk it to death!"

"I'm not," she said. "I'm making sure I understood." She

tasted the wine again. "It's very nice. Thank you." And she sipped more wine. "If your part of France isn't Burgundy, what is it?" And for the rest of lunch, he told her about the slopes that rise eastward out of the Rhône Valley.

Returning to her office after lunch, she'd caught herself humming. And it was back then, that same day, that she'd found it easy finally to accept Snaith's often made suggestion that she call him by his first name.

20

The Mansfield Public Library was a relatively small but ponderous-appearing building of the thick-walled, high-ceilinged, narrow-windowed type often erected during the time of—and possibly as monuments to—William McKinley. Although the day was hot, the unairconditioned interior was livably temperate. Marc and Laura walked to the counter, behind which a woman stood talking on a phone, while two others at a double desk behind the counter were typing on small white index cards. To their left, and just beyond the L-shaped extension of the desk, was a glass-topped display case under which several books were opened to wood engravings. This was the display case which—in its presently-to-be-altered state—would appear in TV news clips and on some front pages.

"I know, Mrs. Dixon," the woman on the phone was saying, "it certainly is our job to help you locate a book you want. But

if all you remember is that it had the word 'affair' in the title
and you think it was written by a woman and you remember
seeing a review of it last spring in either a newspaper or a
magazine. . . ." She rolled her eyes helplessly at Marc and
Laura. "Yes? . . . Oh, it *was* an ad. Did it show the jacket?
. . . Ah, with two heads on it. Men's or women's? . . . A man
and a woman—and a gun . . . Unless it was a knife. Well, look,
Mrs. Dixon, we're closing in a few minutes, but if you'd come
right over, someone would wait and help you go through the
recent fiction . . . You don't want the book? Then why . . . A
word in the title. For a crossword puzzle! Mrs. Dixon. May I
make a suggestion? Why don't you call the Los Angeles Public
Library? You see, it's only morning out there and that would
give them plenty of time—" She slowly replaced the receiver.
"Imagine. She hung up." Then she smiled broadly and Marc
asked, "Is Miss Hester Morehouse in?"

"I am, indeed. Are you Mr. Holland?"

"And Miss Conroy. Of Tabard Press."

"Welcome. Let's go into the office. The others should be
along soon."

They followed her past some stacks and down a corridor
lined by magazine shelves. Hester was a tall, angular woman.
Her short, mannish hair was white. She walked with the long
stride of a woman who would have preferred wearing slacks.
The library's office was a fair-sized, quite cluttered room.
There were desks for four workers, shelves crammed with
catalogues and buying guides, stacked copies of trade and library periodicals. Two opened Coca-Cola bottles and a sickly
African-violet plant were on one of the three window sills. A
large floor fan was doing a feeble air-circulating job.

Hester motioned them to wooden folding chairs and
perched on the edge of a desk, swinging one long leg. "You're
both from New York?"

Marc nodded. Laura said, "I am now. I come from southern
Ohio."

"Oh," said Hester. "I'm from northern Kentucky. Used to

go up to Cincinnati to see the Reds play. Where in southern Ohio?"

"Ludgrove," said Laura. And to Hester's questioning look, "Yes. Same Conroy. Same family, anyhow. Jessica is my mother."

"Hmm." She looked at Marc, then back to Laura. "I take it you're on the library's side of this. Won't you find it embarr—"

Laura broke in. "Not a bit. I've no part of the A.C.E. In fact, for a moment, I was tempted to appear as a witness against them."

Hester turned her surprise toward Marc. He said, "Not against them as much as for Tabard Press—and you." He indicated the library with a wave. "But I doubt her testimony would be held relevant. Anyhow, she's not going to oppose her mother publicly. Now, what can you tell me about *your* opposition?"

Hester slid off the desk and into a chair. "Locally," she said, "it's a brother and sister. The Apsemonts. They both live here in Mansfield. He's an assistant comptroller of an insurance company in Newark. She breeds and shows Afghans. Together, they're the spirit of Anthony Comstock. They're always snooping around the library to see if any books which they consider dirty are in reach of children. They led the local fight against sex education, against the abortion bill and—twenty years ago—they damn near stopped the fluoridation of the reservoir. They're both members of the A.C.E. and she's vice-president of the Jersey chapter. The president is a man you may have heard of—Joe Stegma of Trenton."

"The wholesale-produce man," Marc said. "Wasn't his name mentioned in that market scandal last year?"

"That's Stegma, all right," confirmed Hester. "His name *always* gets mentioned. Especially by district attorneys. But they never manage to pin enough on him to make it stick in front of a grand jury."

"Hmmm," mused Marc. "Funny he should be an A.C.E. type."

"You wouldn't think it very funny if you lived here. He's a real pain to every library and bookstore in the state. Joe Stegma doesn't know much about books, but he sure as hell knows what he doesn't like. And what he doesn't like, he calls 'dirty.' "

"How has your local press reacted to the injunction?"

"Our local press," said Hester, "is *The Channel.* It's a weekly and a lot more concerned with what the supermarket is pushing than with who's pushing who around. They're not unfriendly—in a pantywaist way. They just ran an editorial meant to support me by saying that they're sure my inclusion of *Ecstatic Excursions* in the Invitation to Reading display was an oversight. I've just fired back a letter to the editor telling him it was goddamn deliberate and that the publicity he's given the book will hopefully make it necessary to put in a second copy when the injunction is lifted."

"Does your attorney think that's wise?"

"My attorney thinks it's extremely wise not to interfere with my freedom of expression. Or anyone else's. That's why he's my attorney." She slumped deeper into her chair. "Of course, the J.L.A. thinks I'm picking the wrong moment to shoot my mouth off out of court."

"The J.L.A.?" asked Laura.

"The Jersey Library Association. They've always rallied round. I don't think we'd have an effective system without them. But they're always preaching strategy to me. And I guess they're right. Only, I'm not the strategic type. I act. Then, if there's any time left over, I think about it." She turned her head as two women entered the room. One was short, stout and wearing a linen suit of such simplicity as could only have been cut by a master couturier. The other woman was equally stout, but a head taller. She might once have cared about her appearance—way back in the late fifties when the shapeless garment she was wearing would have been in fashion. The shorter woman turned out to be a Mrs. Laurens or Lawrence and, later, actually a Mrs. Laurens Lawrence with an assured air of social supremacy and the first name of Edna.

The taller woman was Miss Hilda Banks, assistant to the head-mistress of a local private academy for girls.

With the arrival of these members of the board, Hester led them all out of the office toward a stair and down into a basement room that could have accommodated at least ten times as large a group as finally assembled. There were, it turned out, only seven on the Library Board.

21

The basement room was even cooler than the library office. The five of them ignored the slightly elevated stage and podium, and pulled some of the folding chairs below it into a rough circle. They were still scraping the chairs around on the matting-covered cement floor when two men came down the stairs. One was a portly black in his early forties, mustached and balding, who greeted Hilda Banks and Mrs. Lawrence with restraint, Hester with friendly ease and accepted Marc's and Laura's handshakes as Hester introduced him as Mr. Charles Forney. The other man was older and sparer, grave-faced and stiffly proper. He turned out to be Morley Oliver, the board's chairman. Marc remembered him and added to Hester's introduction for Laura's benefit: "Mr. Oliver is head of the educational channel in Jersey, WLLD." "Was head," corrected Oliver, "I'm out to pasture now."

The next arrival was Edgar Dorman, a rather tall and thin man in his early fifties who eventually turned out to be the owner of Dorman's, the only department store in town. A scrap of joking conversation between him and Charles Forney suggested that the latter was a labor leader involved with some union of local importance.

The last two of the seven board members arrived in rapid succession. Flora Gordon Wise was brusque, authoritative, blondly handsome, in her late thirties and subsequently identified as an art director of *Cosmopolitan*. Although they had never met him, neither Marc nor Laura needed introduction to the seventh board member. Still broadly, athletically, erect in what must have been his early seventies, Paul De Witt was instantly recognizable to them. They'd seen his jutting, deeply lined yet gentle face in book-review sections, on thoughtful TV discussion programs and on the jacket of his now classic biography, *Samuel Adams: Portrait of a Protester.* Paul De Witt had moved to a farm on the outskirts of Mansfield after his retirement, eight years before, as one of Princeton's deans. Since shortly thereafter, he'd been a member of the Library Board and an amused and amusing observer and encourager of Hester's more establishment-needling activities.

Morley Oliver said, "We're all here; let's begin. This isn't a regular meeting, so I guess we can dispense with minutes and old business. Hester, we know why you called us, but maybe you should review it."

"Yes. Gladly. You know that the town attorney"—she glanced at Marc—"that's Lew Lahey—has asked for an injunction against the display and circulation of *Ecstatic Excursions.* Judge Negley issued a temporary injunction and ordered me as librarian to show cause in court next Tuesday why it shouldn't be made permanent. Lahey has also accused me of circulating a book contrary to the state obscenity statute and has named Tabard Press, as distributor, co-defendant. I don't know whether the injunction and the case against Tabard and me will be heard at the same time. But, either way, I intend to fight the injunction and defend my innocence." She looked around at them. "The reason I've requested this meeting is to give you a formal opportunity to decide whether I do so as an individual or as your librarian. In other words, I'm giving you a chance to fire me."

Morley Oliver started to say something, but Hester interrupted. "There's something else you should know. Jay Meeker tells me that this kind of complaint is usually handled by the complainant going quietly to the Library Board and trying to persuade enough of its members to remove the book they're objecting to from the shelves."

"I don't know why they didn't do that," said Hilda Banks, "instead of making this public fuss."

"Because they want a public fuss," said Hester. "According to the C.L.U. people that Jay has been in touch with, there are several other cases like this around the country—all in the last few days and all against Tabard Press books. And in every instance, they've begun with temporary injunctions. Someone is out to get Tabard, and to do it with the utmost publicity— Jay calls it an attempt to hurt the publisher's reputation, not just his books." She paused. "Anyhow, that seems to be why they've gone after this injunction which challenges us, or at least me, to an open 'show-cause' hearing, with whatever attendant publicity, next week." She looked around the group. "Not that I'm afraid of the publicity. But maybe you'd have preferred them to have approached you. If they had, and if you'd agreed to removal of the book—I'm sure you know that it would have meant removing me, too. So that's why I'm giving you this chance to let me go."

"Now, Hester," said Morley Oliver in his most soothing chairman-of-the-board manner, "let's not get excited."

"I'm not," said Hester. "I'm just trying to put the issue simply—and fully."

"But you never allow for any compromise," said Hilda Banks as though gently chiding one of her academy's girls. "You always make everything so—so—"

"So black-and-white," suggested Charles Forney.

"Yes," said Hilda, "so bl— Oh, I'm sorry."

"What about?" asked Forney.

Paul De Witt chuckled. "That's what it is. And so is our position. Very clearly, black-and-white."

"Paul," said Flora Gordon Wise, "you sound as though we'd voted already."

"Which we have," said De Witt. "That Invitation to Reading exhibit has been there for more than a year. And *Ecstatic Excursions* has been part of it from the beginning. Regardless of what you may think of the book as an anthology of literature —and for my part, Cabell was the only one of the four who had genuine literary talent—we tacitly accepted and approved its presence. If we back down now, we'd be betraying Hester. To say nothing of the First Amendment."

"Of course, we're not going to let Hester down," Hilda Banks protested. "I mean, you're right that we all knew that book was there. But that was before people objected to it."

"*People* didn't object to it," snapped Hester, "the Apsemonts did. And they aren't people, they're a—a two-headed monolith."

"Well," soothed Morley Oliver, "I guess Hilda means they represent some people."

"They represent a little group of bigots whom they don't usually even bother to consult. When the Apsemonts shout 'Dirty!' their handful of local A.C.E. members go '*Eeee!*' "Hester stretched her long legs in front of her and crossed her ankles. "Anyhow, that's not the point. I think the board has to decide whether to back me or fire me." She pulled her legs back and prepared to rise. "And maybe I ought to go upstairs for a while and give you a chance to talk it over."

"Now, Hester," said Mrs. Lawrence, "that shouldn't be necessary." She turned to Hilda. "You said something before about compromise. What did you mean?"

Hilda plucked at her skirt. "Well, as I say, we can't refuse to back Hester. But maybe we should say—now that our attention has been called to the dubious nature of that book—that we should just withdraw it. Very quietly. Then everybody will be happy."

"I won't!" snapped Hester.

"Hilda," said Paul De Witt, "not that I think it has anything to do with the matter, but why do you consider that book's nature dubious?"

"Well, it *has* sex scenes. And . . . I haven't actually read it, but some of the girls at the school were giggling about the—about some of the words in it. You know, four-letter ones."

"Are you suggesting," asked Flora Gordon Wise, "that they hadn't encountered those words before?"

"Well, I don't know . . ."

"Don't you ever go to the ladies' room? Not the faculty one. The 'Girls'?"

Hilda straightened. "I wouldn't invade their privacy."

"Good for you!" said Flora. "But maybe you ought to learn more about their contemporary speech and graffiti."

"When was this giggling?" asked De Witt. "Back in the spring, before school closed?"

"Oh no, we're having a short summer make-up session. It was just the other day—yesterday. When the paper came out about the injunction. One of the girls must have found or bought a copy of the book—or something."

"And you'd never heard them mention the book before the injunction?"

"Why, no."

Paul sat back and smiled across at Marc.

Charles Forney stirred. "Have you"—he was looking at Flora—"read the fourth novel in that book? The new one, *Miss Baker's Dozen?*"

"No," said Flora, "I haven't. But I'm sure I've read others like it. Why? Have you read it, Charles?"

"Yes, I read it. And I'd hate to have my daughter read it. Or yours either, Flora."

"But they're only seven," said Hester. "Children don't browse or borrow in that section."

"I mean when she grows up," said Forney. "When she's as old as the older girls in Hilda Banks' school. That's about fifteen, sixteen, isn't it?"

Hilda nodded.

Charles continued, "The language in that book is ghetto language. I know. Is that what we want for the children in this town?"

"Charles," said De Witt, "it isn't necessarily what we want for anyone anywhere. But that language isn't any more ghetto than it's country-club. It's the vernacular. And almost all of it has a rich linguistic base." He turned to Laura. "Miss Conroy, you don't look so old as to be likely to have forgotten your mid-teens. You knew that language then, didn't you?"

Laura hesitated. "I—I'd heard it. And seen some of it. But I didn't know it too well. But I think mine was a special case. I'm—I'm a late learner."

Marc glanced swiftly sidewise at her. Then he turned to the group. "What you're talking about is the heart of this case, or at least of the defense. The New Jersey obscenity statute says a book—or picture, or public performance—is obscene if the average person, applying contemporary community stand-ards, finds its dominant theme or purpose is an appeal to prurient interest. I think that's what you're talking about right now—contemporary community standards."

"In my day," said De Witt, "I seem to recall something about 'redeeming social value.'"

"There was," said Marc. "And still is. But not in this state any longer. Nor in a couple of others, and—if A.C.E. has its way—in the whole country pretty soon."

"But isn't redeeming social value in the Constitution?" asked Morley Oliver.

Marc shook his head. "It never was. The Constitution merely says that Congress shall make no law abridging— among other things—freedom of the press. It wasn't until 1957 in *Roth v. U.S.* that the Supreme Court decided that something is obscene if it is utterly without redeeming social value—I think the term was 'social importance'—*and* its dominant theme appeals to prurient interests *and* it affronts contempo-rary community standards. Most states, including this one, made their obscenity laws conform to that decision. But now this state has struck out the first part." Marc shrugged. "Of course, this new and narrower state law may be found unconstitutional by the Supreme Court." He paused and reflected. "Or maybe made more repressive."

Edgar Dorman spoke for the first time. "Then what you're saying is that the town attorney will have to prove that this book goes beyond our present community standards."

Marc nodded. "As applied by the average person."

"Hmm," mused De Witt. "Doesn't that mean that he'll have to find an average person?"

"It probably means that *we* will. He'll likely as not just submit the book and let people like the Apsemonts state their objections."

"Can he, or they, point out individual words and passages?"

"I'm sure they'll try. And we'll object. We'll demand that the work be considered as a whole. Then it's up to the judge —and maybe, later on, an appeals court." Marc leaned forward. "Naturally, we'll present average people who will testify that the book doesn't offend them or community standards as they understand them."

"So," said De Witt, "*we* have to find average people. I wonder if they exist."

"You don't think so, Paul?" asked Morley Oliver.

"I doubt it. I think the average person is a mythical concept derived from adding up all the extraordinarily individual people in the world and dividing by their total number. I don't even think Miss Apsemont or her brother represents an average of the two of them. Each is different—by hormones if by nothing else."

"They have none," said Hester bitterly. "Anyhow, all this comes later. When we, or I, consider the defense of this case. Right now, I'm asking you to decide which it will be. Me on my own, or me as your librarian?"

"There certainly can't be any question about that," said Flora Gordon Wise. "You *are* our librarian. And *we* are defending this case against you."

"Is that a motion?" asked Morley Oliver.

"It is."

"Do I hear a second?"

After a brief pause De Witt, who seemed to have been waiting to see who else might speak, said, "I second."

Oliver looked around. "Any discussion?"

Edgar Dorman asked, "Have we any idea what defending this case might cost? I mean the library budget . . ."

Charles Forney said, "I was wondering about that, too."

"It's refreshing," said De Witt, "to find business and labor on the same side of a money issue."

Mrs. Lawrence started to say, "I'm sure there are several of us who would be glad to contribute—"

"It won't be necessary," Hester cut in. "The Civil Liberties Union is defraying Jay Meeker's fee."

"They're not all that rich," said De Witt. "In fact, they're pretty much always strapped. After this motion is passed—as I trust it will be—perhaps we can consider the possibility of the Library Fund *and* some private contributors joining with the C.L.U. in paying the costs."

"I wouldn't welcome that idea," said Mrs. Lawrence. "I'd prefer not to associate with the C.L.U. After the way they defended those student demonstrators down at Rutgers."

"That," said De Witt, "is one reason I suggest our sharing their expense. Anyhow, that's another issue. I move the question, Morley."

"Yes," said Flora, "let's get on with it."

The question was put. There were no noes. But it wasn't certain that everyone had voted aye.

22

From the library, Hester took Marc and Laura to Jay Meeker's office in Morristown. De Witt drove them, explaining that his elderly station wagon could better accommodate them all than Hester's VW or Marc's rented compact and that, anyway, he wanted them to come back to his farm for drinks in the late afternoon. Marc and Laura were delighted to have more of his company; Hester wasn't at all surprised by his suggestion—she knew De Witt's preference for the companionship of young people, especially when an attractive young girl was among them.

Jay's office was on the second floor of a professional building. It was closed on Saturday, but he'd opened it for the meeting with Marc. Jay was a bristly-haired, gnarled man not unlike a younger version of De Witt. He and Marc agreed that their chief problem was to produce some "average persons," and Jay, who'd already begun the search, promised to find a few representatives of different age groups and social classes. They also agreed that the town attorney would try to introduce, and would probably succeed in doing so, the fact that *Miss Baker's Dozen* included passages written by someone else to relieve its sexual concentration.

"There's a very remote possibility," said Mark, "that the complaint may be withdrawn." When Jay looked startled, he went on, "Miss Conroy has written her mother that she might appear as a witness for the defense. Actually, she's not going to. But she thinks her mother might decide to keep her name out of this."

"And if Mrs. Conroy doesn't withdraw?" He turned to Laura. "What then?"

"Do you think it would be helpful if I appeared?"

"To say what?"

"To say that I'm now doing the kind of collaborative writing that Judy Cuneo did. And to give my reasons for thinking it's right and proper."

"But Miss Cuneo could say that."

Laura shrugged. "Maybe not the way I could. To Judy, it was just a job. But I've thought a lot about it, or at least listened to a lot about it. I might be more—well, more earnest maybe . . ." Her voice trailed off indecisively. "Opposing Mother like that, in public—I might get too nervous."

"It may not even be admissible," said Jay. "After all, you're not involved in the book before the court."

"I told her that," Marc said.

Jay turned to Hester. "Anyhow, if Miss Conroy were to appear and the local paper tied her in with her mother, that would probably give the case more publicity than—"

"I'm not afraid of publicity," said Hester. "I can take it. I'm not so sure the Apsemont types can. They might look pretty silly. After all, they're picking on some pretty feeble soft-core porn." She turned back to Laura. "Three quarters of that anthology lost its potency years ago."

"But it's the other quarter," Jay reminded her, "that they're objecting to. *That*, they claim, is pretty hard-core."

"Hah!" exclaimed Hester. "That's pallid stuff, too. I doubt it could ever arouse anyone, except the Apsemonts. And I'll bet all he can get up is his eyebrows."

23

A dozen years before, when the De Witts had bought the house on the hillside outside of Mansfield, it had been a snug fit for them and their children. And when the boy and his sisters married and moved away, it became suddenly far roomier than Paul and his wife required. At the beginning of the seventies, Paul became a widower and nearly sold the place as an absurdity for himself and the housekeeper, who drove over daily from Plainfield. Then Paul's elder son-in-law, the archaeologist, got his teaching post at Douglas, so one of Paul's girls came home again, complete with husband and two small children. Paul gladly turned the house over to them. All he wanted was their company, his big study, and any one of the bedrooms they didn't need.

Now, in the summer of '72, Paul was temporarily alone again. Daughter, son-in-law and grandchildren were in Yucatán working a Mayan dig which the pair had helped get started nearly a decade earlier on their honeymoon. Paul was a gregarious man and he had several worlds of company to choose from: academia, publishing, and then the whole miscellany of people whose friendship he'd acquired along the varied pathways of his life. These friends ranged from a husband and wife who were famous and untraditional sociologists to a witty woman who had, years before, been a celebrated stripper. Of the local people, Hester was one of his favorites. He loved to make her vigorous, one-sided opinions burn fiercer by stoking them with deliberate, challenging examinations of the other side of whatever cause she happened to be espousing.

When Paul and his wife had bought the house, one of the features which particularly attracted them was its pre-Revolution origin. Wings and porches had been added over the past two and a half centuries, but the central structure was still borne on the original adzed beams, and many of its window frames still held the homemade bottle-bottom glass that its eighteenth-century builder had set.

When they arrived late that Saturday afternoon, at Hester's urging they toured the house, lingering longest in Paul's study. Its four walls were lined with crammed, floor-to-ceiling bookshelves which also ran above the windows and the door. One wall, directly behind his broad heavy oak worktable, was filled with a writer's reference books and several hundred volumes of American history. This and English literature had been Paul's teaching specialties and the subject of most of his writing. The rest of his library was unspecialized, casually arranged and reflective only of Paul's catholicity of taste. The fiction ranged from the classic to the farthest-out experimental. The plays reached back to Aeschylus and forward into the world-beyond-Brecht. There was poetry and philosophy, personal narrative and biography. Perhaps one in ten of his modern volumes was personally, often gratefully, inscribed. The total collection was tiny in public-library terms but its contents made Hester's mouth water, although its haphazard arrangement threatened to topple her Dewey-decimaled mind.

Paul's knowledge of history had been more than echoed by his wife. She, too, had taught. Her two-volume study of the Pre-Raphaelites had been at least as well researched as any work of Paul's, and many critics had found her writing subtler and more exquisite than anything he had done—other than a literary biography of Defoe, an early work bearing all the earmarks of a labor of love. Paul's wife had extended an interest in Americana into the world of antiques, and their home held a wealth of her collecting. One of these was a bed. It stood in what was now a guest room—a lovely fourposter whose spooled uprights were tall enough to carry—as once it doubtless had—a canopy. It might well be of museum quality. As Paul explained, his wife had stumbled on it at an auction sale near Morristown and had devoted odd moments of her ensuing several years to a search for just the right crocheted spread.

When they came down to the screened porch beyond his library, Paul, making drinks, was still talking about the bed, but in the context of the day's earlier meetings.

"Naturally, it's been photographed many times. You'll find it in several coffee-table books on American furniture. Every once in a while I hear from a dealer who has a customer. But I treasure it too much. And it fascinates me. Especially the fact that we know so much, and so little, about it."

"How can it be both ways?" asked Laura.

"Mores, my dear. Mores. Back in the century when that bed was first used they wrote and published almost everything concerning it. Its design, its workmanship, its antecedents and descendants, the fabrics which canopied and covered it, the people who used it. But they left out the heart of the matter: How was it used?"

"Why, Paul," said Hester, "you're becoming a sexual historian."

"Nope. I'm continuing to be a social one." He was passing drinks around. "We may guess that it was used—other than for sleep—discreetly, modestly, in a manner prescribed by the tenets of the time . . . but that's only an assumption. We know that it might occasionally have held a bundling board—it's grooved for one—but we still don't know for sure whether such low obstacles were effective devices or merely polite symbols. Some might say, 'Of what possible importance is it to know how often or in what variety it was sexually employed?' but a social historian needs all the evidence he can get to measure, for instance, whether the propriety of the time was merely outward show or deep-veined repression. Two hundred years hence, historians will know such things about us, thanks to the relative freedom of expression we are now enjoying and in spite of Apsemont-type efforts to suppress that freedom and expunge its record."

"Then," said Marc, "it's mainly as a historian that you defend erotica?"

"Not quite. I defend it, and its more pornographic forms as well, primarily because it *is* expression, harms no one—though one gets frequent arguments on that score—and also because it does record a way (not necessarily *the* way) of behaving in this day. A twenty-second-century historian, finding the best or the worst of our current erotica may, without enough other evidence, confuse imaginings with realities and reach a false conclusion about the prevalence of our varied sexuality." Paul went back to his little bar and stirred himself a sour mash and water. "But at least he'll be able to say, 'They could print and publish that then.'"

He turned toward his guests. "Whether he says it as one long-accustomed to such literature or as one coming upon a relic of forgotten freedom depends on us."

He sat on a low couch between Laura and Hester. "This liberty, too, depends on eternal vigilance."

24

The Guernsey County Courthouse in Mansfield, New Jersey, seemed to have been struck from the same architectural mold that had given birth to the Mansfield Public Library. McKinley appeared to have left a lasting imprint on more than American Pacific policy.

Judge Katherine Negley was a "club house" judge. She'd come up through the local Democratic machine, had served two terms in the State Legislature, been an assistant district attorney for Guernsey and been appointed to her seat on the bench three years before. Meanwhile she'd raised four small children into their early teens, and nowadays avoided hearing actions involving her husband's sizable construction company. This meant disqualifying herself in a considerable number of cases, as the Negley-Riccio people had a lamentable record of dropping things on and running over people.

When the town attorney, Lew Lahey, had appeared in court the week before, accompanied by the Apsemonts and bearing a library copy of *Ecstatic Excursions*, Judge Negley listened to the complaint, glanced through the cited fourth novel in the omnibus, *Miss Baker's Dozen*, and quickly decided that she should hear arguments why the book should not be banned from the library and that, meanwhile, a temporary restraint on its display and circulation could work no irreparable harm on the book, the library or the public. Her quick legal eye having caught a few sentences from a part of the novel wherein Miss Baker becomes embroiled with a gendarme and a parboiled tongue, she had remanded the book to her own custody until the show-cause hearing—on this sultry Tuesday.

It was a quarter to eleven and the courtroom's lazy ceiling fans had by now demonstrated their inability to stir the cloying atmosphere. Lew Lahey had completed restating the community's case against the book and was extracting the testimony of Jerrold Apsemont, Complainant.

Apsemont should have been a jovial man. His face was round, his body rounder. He could easily have been cast as the benign uncle who cherished his annual role as Santa Claus for his nephews and nieces. But those who could identify his sister and only sibling, Mildred, knew from her flat and forbidding body and ringless fingers that no blood relative would ever call him uncle. Nor was it likely that anything so suggestive as a stocking would ever grace a mantel in the house they shared.

"You have, then, read the book, *Ecstatic Excursions?*" asked Lew rhetorically.

"Yes," said Apsemont in what should have been a resonant voice but which, considering his breadth and height, was unpleasantly tenor. "At one time or another."

"Perhaps you had better clarify that."

"Three of the novels in it were published a long time ago. I can't say when I read *Jurgen* or how much of it I read. The same is true of *Replenishing Jessica* and *Aphrodite.* I can be more precise about *Miss Baker's Dozen.* I read that in its original paperback form year before last when it was published."

"And what— I withdraw that for the moment." Lew moved back toward his table. "You've already identified yourself as an employee of an insurance company. You're in the financial end, I believe."

"Yes. I'm in the comptroller's department."

"And you are a resident of Mansfield?"

"Yes."

"How long have you lived here?"

"I was born in Mansfield. In the house where my sister and I live now."

"Do you belong to any clubs or organizations in Mansfield?"

"I'm not eligible for the service clubs because I'm not a local businessman. I belong to a church here and I teach in the Sunday School."

"How would you place yourself in the local social and economic scale?"

"About in the middle, I guess. I'm not well-to-do. But I earn enough for my needs. Between that and what my sister usually can count on from her Afghan breeding—we're comfortable."

Judge Negley glanced over at Jay Meeker and said, "A stipulation that Mr. Apsemont is an average person as defined in the obscenity statute might speed things up."

Jay rose. "We'd just as soon the town attorney continued, Your Honor."

Judge Negley sighed and motioned to Lew, who shrugged and moved toward his witness. "Do you go to the movies?"

"Occasionally."

"And you read books?"

"When I have time."

"You visit friends—they visit you?"

"Oh yes."

Lew addressed the bench. "Your Honor, as you correctly observed, the Town is establishing the witness as an average person. Even though the defense appears reluctant to stipulate, perhaps I needn't proceed further into whether he goes bowling, watches television, and so forth. There being no jury, it is perhaps not improper for me to observe that he does these things and more in the area of average, normal activity. If the court so desires, I'll pursue that line further." He paused and looked at the judge. She looked at Jay. He looked at the ceiling. The judge said, "If it becomes necessary, you may reopen that line later."

"Thank you, Your Honor." Lew turned back to Apsemont. "Do you know of any reason why you should not consider yourself an average person in this average New Jersey community?"

Jay started to rise, then sank back. Apsemont answered, "No, sir."

"Do you," continued Lew, "consider yourself aware of this community's contemporary standards?"

This time Jay made it fully to his feet. "Objection. No effort has been made to establish the witness's competence in this area."

"As an average, intelligent citizen—" Lew began.

"The first point may not have been proved. The second point hasn't even been introduced."

Judge Negley pursed her lips. "I'll sustain," she said.

Jay sat and Lew returned to Apsemont. "What was your education?"

"I graduated from Mansfield High and took a Bachelor of Business Science at Rutgers—the Newark branch."

"Do you read the local paper?"

"Yes."

"What magazines do you read?"

"*U.S. News and World Report, Reader's Digest, Nation's Business.* Also the *Eastern Underwriter* and other insurance trade journals."

"Have you read classical literature?"

"I've read Shakespeare. And *A Tale of Two Cities.* A lot of books which don't come to mind right away."

"In your business, are you called upon to make judgments of people—estimating their value, their competence, their character and standards?"

"I have to. I hire and fire the people under me."

"Thank you. Now I repeat the earlier question. As an average man with the intelligence to judge people and events, do you consider yourself aware of this community's standards?"

Jay was on his feet again. "Your Honor, I don't want to prolong this hearing. Instead of making an objection, may I observe for the record that the witness has not been qualified as a sociologist, a social researcher, or even as possessing average standards?"

The judge nodded and motioned to Lew to continue.

"You have read the novel *Miss Baker's Dozen* contained in the volume *Ecstatic Excursions?*"

"I have."

"What is your opinion of it?"

"It is a filthy piece of hard-core pornography solely intended to arouse the prurient interests of its readers."

"Does it conform to contemporary community standards?"

"Certainly not. No more than the graffiti on the walls of the bus-station washroom does."

"Could this novel in this volume do harm, in your opinion?"

"It could do massive harm. It could inflame, arouse, pervert and dehumanize its readers."

"Thank you." Lew walked back to his table and nodded to Jay.

Jay went toward the witness chair, then turned to the judge. "Your Honor, I'll begin this cross examination, but under the permission granted by you at the outset, Mr. Holland may step in."

The judge said, "Yes. Mr. Lahey made no objection."

"We're grateful to both of you." He faced the witness. "Mr. Apsemont. Are you perverted?"

"I beg your pardon!"

"Did *Miss Baker's Dozen* pervert you?"

"No. Of course not."

"Did it dehumanize you?"

Apsemont shook his head in annoyance. "Certainly not."

"Did it, at the time you read it, inflame or arouse you?"

"No!"

"Why not? You've testified that it has the evil power to accomplish all of these miracles."

"Not on *me.*"

"Why not? Aren't you an average person?"

"Yes. But I'm no longer young and impressionable."

"Then I assume you wish to modify your previous testimony."

"Not at all," said Apsemont. "I said it *could* do massive harm. And it could, to those not proof against it."

"Are most people proof against it?"

"I don't think so. And certainly not young people."

"When you say young people—what age group do you have in mind?"

"People under the middle twenties, students, radicals, all the impressionistic kids."

"You, I assume, are well beyond that age—perhaps in your forties or so?"

"I am."

"Are you a sociologist?"

"No."

"Have you read or studied extensively in that field?" Jay turned toward his table and picked up a sheaf of papers as though prepared to question from them.

"No. Not especially."

"Do you know that more than half the population is now under twenty-five?"

Apsemont shook his head.

"Do you still consider yourself average?"

"I consider myself more than— I certainly do consider myself average. And I've become something of an expert in this field."

"In this field of what you call pornography?"

"Yes."

Jay went back to the defense table and sat on its edge. "Mr. Apsemont. Tell us about your reading. Other than Shakespeare and Dickens. What pornography have you read?"

"As a member of Americans for Clean Entertainment, I've made it my unpleasant duty to read as much of it as I could get my hands on."

Laura, sitting behind the rail separating the court from the spectators, had been watching him with distaste. At the mention of A.C.E., she winced.

"Very good," said Jay. "Now, tell us, are there gradations of pornography?"

"How do you mean?"

"One hears of hard-core and soft-core, of erotica—can you, as an expert, tell us of the differences between them?"

"Hard-core is sold surreptitiously. Under the counter. Soft-core is sold brazenly out in the open. Erotica is a general term without much meaning to me."

"Well, let's imagine two books. Let's say one had been sold openly and the other from under the counter. But you don't know which one. Now, let's say you've read them both. Could you then tell which was which?"

"The under-the-counter stuff is often sadistic, for instance."

"Like the works of De Sade himself?"

"Yes."

"But *they're* sold out in the open. There's no objection to *them.*"

"*I* object to them."

Jay nodded. "Now, this book, *Miss Baker's Dozen*. When it was published separately as a Solus book by Tabard Press, how was it sold?"

"From paperback racks."

"These weren't under the counter, were they?"

"No. They were out in the open."

"And no action was taken against this book in New Jersey or in any other state—as far as you know?"

"No." Apsemont hesitated. "That was before the state obscenity statute was changed."

"Meanwhile, the book had not become any more objectionable?"

"Not any less, either."

"To you?"

"To lots of people."

"But the fact is that this book has been sold openly since its publication several years ago?"

"Yes."

"Would you accept the statement"—Jay reached around to the table and picked up a small memo-sized piece of paper— "that according to the local wholesaler handling Solus books out here, a hundred copies of that book have been distributed in Guernsey County? And that few have yet been returned, unsold?"

Apsemont put on his most pained expression. "It wouldn't surprise me. The public appetite for filth is huge."

Jay let the paper float back to the table. "Now, since that book was published and distributed, could you furnish us with the names of a few people from this area—three, four, maybe a half dozen—who have been aroused, inflamed, perverted or dehumanized by this book?"

Lew was on his feet. "Objection! The witness testified to what he considered the general effect of the book. Not to specific instances of its effect."

Jay turned from the witness, waving his question away. "Maybe Mr. Holland has a question."

Marc rose behind the table. "I, too, thank the court and the prosecutor for this opportunity." He walked around the table. "Mr. Apsemont, earlier you mentioned reading Shakespeare. Have you read him extensively?"

Apsemont relaxed. "Not all the plays. But some of them quite a lot."

"Hamlet? Macbeth?"

Apsemont waved a fat hand. "Oh, of course. And many others."

"Do you consider them dirty—pornographic?"

"Shakespeare? Oh, you mean some of those vulgarisms in the crowd scenes and from the nurse in *Romeo and Juliet.* No. Not dirty."

"Did you know that in the past they have been so considered?"

Apsemont nodded. "I suppose you're talking about Bowdler. The silly man who put out a cleaned-up edition of Shakespeare a couple of centuries ago."

"Do you approve of his having done that?"

"No, I don't. Shakespeare is classical, his works weren't intended to arouse illicit passions."

"Are you sure? His Elizabethan audiences were pretty lusty in their entertainment demands."

Lew rose. "Isn't the defense straying pretty far from the issue?"

"I'll get to it, Your Honor." The judge, who had leaned forward, sank back again, and Marc walked to the witness stand offering a sheet of paper.

"Will you examine this list of private secondary schools, Mr. Apsemont?"

Apsemont read slowly down the sheet.

"Do you recognize the names of any of those schools?"

"Yes. I've heard of quite a few."

"How would you characterize them—the ones you've heard of?"

"Very fine. Expensive, I think, and exclusive, private academies." Apsemont studied the list further. "Mostly for girls, I believe."

"Mr. Apsemont, I assure you that every one of those schools permits the reading of no Shakespeare except in the bowdlerized edition. Take my word for it. Otherwise I can easily produce proof. Now, tell me, what do you think of deleting, from a copy of *Hamlet* being studied, such a line as 'Do you think I meant country matters?' "

"Why would anyone, even Bowdler, object to that?"

"Because," said Marc, "Hamlet says it while reclining with his head in Ophelia's lap and the line contains an Elizabethan pun on the female genitalia."

Apsemont blanched. "What! But how dare you—" He glanced at Judge Negley. "There are ladies present."

The judge said, "The court can take care of itself. You may answer the question."

Apsemont looked bewildered.

"I'll rephrase it," said Marc. "What do you think of minds which forbid such Shakespearean lines to be read in school?"

"In girls' schools," Apsemont reminded him.

"Yes," said Marc. "What do you think of such minds?"

"I don't know. I mean, that's inexcusable language . . . if that's what it means." He became firm. "I think the schools are justified."

"Then Bowdler wasn't a—what did you call him—a silly man?"

Lew was up again. "Your Honor, this has nothing whatever to do with the book before the court."

"Your Honor," said Marc, "I believe Mr. Apsemont's newfound agreement with a long-discredited eighteenth-century prig has a great deal to do with Mr. Apsemont's qualifications as an estimator and upholder of contemporary community standards. Those schools, incidentally, are—as the witness points out—celebrated. But most of them are more famous for their discipline in etiquette than in the arts and sciences." He paused. "Maybe the witness can find agreement with someone a bit more recent than Bowdler."

He walked back to the table and picked up another note. "Do you go along with the man who said this: 'Shakespeare, Madam, is obscene, and Thank God, *we* are sufficiently advanced to have found it out!' " Marc lowered the note. "In light of your most recent testimony, do you agree with that statement?"

Apsemont shifted his bulk in the witness chair. "Well, from the way he speaks, he sounds pretty far back."

"So do most of the people quoted in the Bible. But I'm sure you agree with *them*. However, I'll tell you that this speaker is from a fairly recent time and a place I believe you've visited as a delegate to conventions—Cincinnati."

"I don't see that I agree or disagree with him. I guess some of Shakespeare is obscene, and some isn't."

"Assuming that to be true, which course would you advocate—to make all of Shakespeare available, or some of it, or none of it?"

"Well, I don't like people to read things like that speech from *Hamlet.*"

"*You've* read it."

"I didn't know what it meant. Neither do most people."

"I see. Then you have no objection to the publication of something that won't be understood. It's knowledge that you seem to take exception to?"

Laura, behind the rail, sat back with a delighted smile.

Lew Lahey was up again. "Your Honor, I object to counsel's interpretation of the testimony. Also, it smacks of trickery to submit a quotation while deliberately concealing its source."

"There's no mystery about its source, Your Honor," said Marc. "It is quoted as having been stated by"—again he read from his note—" 'a gentleman said to be a scholar and a man of reading.' He is further identified as taking part, in Cincinnati in 1828, in a conversation with Mrs. Frances Trollope, who was writing her rather defamatory book, *Domestic Manners of the Americans.*"

Judge Negley said, "I'll sustain the objection. The point seems an obscure one." She paused, then added, "Unless the defense is somehow trying to discredit the city of Cincinnati because it happens to be the headquarters of the organization Mr. and Miss Apsemont represent."

"Actually no, Your Honor," Marc said. "I found that quote in Boyer's *Purity in Print*, and from the same source I learned that the Western Society for the Suppression of Vice was founded in Cincinnati by William Breed in the late eighteen-eighties. But he wasn't a Cincinnatian. He was a native of Massachusetts who came to Cincinnati as a young man and made a fortune. Manufacturing coffins. I'd be glad to concede that far from being a Cincinnati phenomenon, he may have been a traveling representative of the Boston Watch and Ward—"

"Please," Judge Negley interrupted, "you're way beyond the limits of even generous latitude."

Marc dropped the note on the table. "Forgive me, Your Honor. May I have the court's permission to pursue a new line?"

"Yes. Please."

Marc turned almost accusingly to Apsemont. "Do you drink?"

"No. Of course not."

"Not even occasionally?"

"No."

"Do you smoke?"

"No."

"Play cards?"

"I do not."

"You are unmarried, I believe."

Apsemont nodded.

"I know you live with your sister and I imagine delicacy would cause you to go to a motel or the girl's home when you have a date."

Apsemont started to sputter. "I don't—you shouldn't—"

Lew jumped to his feet again. "Your Honor, surely this line of questioning is highly improper."

"If that's an objection," said Judge Negley, "I'll sustain it."

"I apologize, Your Honor," said Marc, "it *was* an improper question. Especially to so proper a man. You see"—he looked at the judge—"I was desperately searching for some ground, any ground, on which Mr. Apsemont could even remotely be considered, in the words of the statute, 'an average person.' "

From the small group of spectators there was a startled laugh, which the judge quickly rapped to silence. Returning to the table, Marc saw Laura looking up at him with smiling eyes. Behind her were several members of the Library Board. Morley Oliver was sitting next to Edna Lawrence. He had laughed; she hadn't. Hilda Banks had a startled expression on her face. Charles Forney was frowning. Just in front of Forney and behind the rail, a young woman was holding a pad on her knee, bending forward and writing on it while her long and bright red hair cascaded around her face. "Who's that taking notes?" asked Marc, nudging Jay.

Jay looked around. "Oh! That's Annie. Anne Semple Cobb, as her by-line in *The Channel* puts it. Her father started the paper; now her husband owns it. She'll probably want to interview you. Tell her as little as possible; it gives her less to embroider."

"Oh."

"And never say 'This is off the record'—that makes it a page-one headline."

Lew Lahey was making a brave salvage attempt on redirect examination, eliciting the fact that Jerrold Apsemont had been summoned as an "average person" in previous obscenity trials and had not successfully been challenged. He did inadvertently open a new issue by extracting the fact that Apsemont also took exception to the other novels in *Ecstatic Excursions* and still considered *Jurgen* a work which the public would be better off not reading. "I'm speaking as a responsible citizen," he said. "I'm not attempting literary criticism."

This gave Marc an opportunity to cross-examine further and to introduce the fact that way back in the late teens of the century, the Chicago *Tribune's* book reviewer had called James Branch Cabell "the greatest living master of English prose."

"Does that statement surprise you?" asked Marc.

"I'm surprised to hear it come from a good conservative newspaper."

"Is that all that surprises you about it?"

"Only that it's said in support of a notorious pornographer."

"But not that it was said when James Joyce was writing?"

"He wrote dirty books, too."

"You are referring to. . . ?"

"*Ulysses.*"

Judge Negley cut in. "We are *not* going to try that case again."

"Certainly not, Your Honor," Marc assured her. "Actually, *Jurgen* was published three years before *Ulysses* at a time when Joyce's major existing works were *Dubliners* and *Portrait of the Artist as a Young Man*—neither of which was ever successfully challenged over here as obscene. We are demonstrating, Your Honor, that the witness is not very familiar with literature."

"Of course not," said Lahey, rising. "He's an average person. He need not be learned in the arts."

Marc said, "We'll agree with the prosecutor on that point. We hope he will agree that an average person might, on the other hand, have considerable learning in the art of literature."

Lew waved a hand. "Oh sure."

"Thank you," said Marc, and again walking back to his table, winked across the railing at Paul De Witt.

At twelve-thirty, Judge Negley adjourned for lunch. Before that, Lahey had called a local housewife whom he qualified as average in various depressing senses and who testified to having read and been shocked by *Miss Baker's Dozen*. Lahey carefully avoided extracting a condemnation of the book and led her no further than making the statement that she found it obscene far beyond community standards. Jay asked her whether she had discussed the book with anyone, her family, her friends, and was delighted to receive her assurance that she wouldn't have *dared* talk about it to anyone. Which gave him the opportunity to ask her how, in that case, she could know how community-wide her opinion might be.

25

The best and worst restaurant in Mansfield's center was crowded. Snaith, Jorgenson and Judy Cuneo joined Jay Meeker at the soda counter. Hester and Paul De Witt found a too-small table for themselves with Marc and Laura.

Hester asked Marc how he thought it was going and Marc thought well enough. He also doubted that they'd finish in this one day. Snaith, who evidently had the same word from Jay, came to their table to tell Marc and Laura they'd probably have to stay overnight. Was there, he asked Hester, an inn or a motel? Paul said there was, but why bother? He could accommodate more than all of them in his near-empty house, especially if some of them doubled up. Snaith said he and Jorgenson could, maybe Judy and Laura . . . He caught Marc's eye and his voice trailed off. "We'll work it out," said Paul. Laura started to say, "I didn't even bring a toothbrush—" And Hester muttered, "There's a drugstore around the corner where you can get most anything you'll need."

When court reconvened at a few minutes after two, Lew Lahey addressed the bench.

"Your Honor, the People at this point would like to in-

troduce testimony to support our contention that the book we
seek to enjoin is not only obscene beyond contemporary community standards, but that its publisher and author know—
and knew—it to be so and sought artificially to inject it with
redeeming social value as a protection for it in those states
where that standard still applies. We know it no longer applies
in New Jersey, but we think this testimony will be relevant as
an admission, by its creator and its purveyor, that it is obscene."

Judge Negley looked inquiringly at the defense table. Jay,
rising, said, "We will not object to such testimony. If it is what
we expect it to be, we welcome it. It will give us an opportunity to try to establish here a precedent which we believe
will be valuable to other defendants against similar prosecu-
tions."

Judge Negley said, "I'm not sure we should take the time for
such a purpose. However, if the prosecutor wishes to proceed
and will endeavor to keep it brief, we will allow this, subject
to a later ruling to strike it."

"Thank you, Your Honor," said Lahey. "The witnesses I
intend to call are associated with the defense. Therefore, I
assume they will be hostile and I request indulgence of leading
questions."

Jay spoke again. "They will not be hostile, Your Honor.
And we won't object to latitude toward leading. It will speed
things up."

"Thank you," said Lew doubtfully. "We call Ralph Jorgenson."

A thin, yet potbellied man of about forty rose and came
through the gate. In front of the witness chair he took the
oath, stated his name and gave an address far west on
Twenty-third Street, New York. Below a thinning hairline,
Jorgenson's brow was broad. He had rather protruberant
eyes and a nose made more prominent by his sallow, sunken
cheeks. When he spoke, his voice was so low as nearly to
rumble.

"Mr. Jorgenson, what is your profession?"

"Mostly I'm a writer. Sometimes I get other odd jobs. In stores. Clerking."

"What do you write?"

"Most anything. I get free-lance assignments to do booklets and pamphlets—like advertising. I've done some pieces for magazines. I write books."

"What kind of books?"

"Novels."

"A special kind of novel—aren't they?"

"Oh, yeah. You mean, erotica?"

"Is that what *you* mean? Are your novels erotic?"

"Well, sure."

"In other words, they're about sexual activity. Right?"

"Right."

"In them, do you describe sexual congress?"

"Oh, yeah."

"Between men and women?"

"Umm. Lots of the time."

"And men and men?"

"Oh, sure."

"Women and women?"

"Yup."

"Are animals ever involved?"

"Not much. That's not my bag."

Lahey walked away, looked at a note on his table and returned. "Do you describe sexual organs?"

"Sure. How else could you write my kind of book?"

"Are these organs in aroused states?"

"Lots of the time. Sometimes before—or even after. Or, you know, not able to."

"Do you describe moments of sexual climax?"

"Well, certainly."

"With details of physical and sensual response?"

"Eh?"

"How they look? How they act? That kind of thing?"

"Oh. Yes. All the senses. Hearing, feeling, seeing, tasting—"

"Thank you. Did you write *Miss Baker's Dozen?*"

"Yes."

"Under the name of Teddy Mario?"

"Yes."

"You didn't want to put your own name on it?"

"No. I keep my own name for the magazine pieces. Some of them are sort of inspirational. They go in mags published by groups that wouldn't like— I mean, I even write for a church mag."

"I see. But Teddy Mario isn't the only name you use? I believe you write under other pseudonyms."

"That's right. I write my novels under several different names."

"Why?"

"Because I write three or four novels a year, and they can't all seem to come from the same guy. The readers wouldn't think I'd spent enough time on them."

"Do you spend enough time?"

"Oh, sure. I can write this sex stuff like a banging rabbit."

"I accept your self-criticism. I presume that one factor contributing to your writing speed is the fact that you don't write the whole book yourself."

"That's true."

"What parts don't you write?"

"The parts that bore me. What's going on between the sex scenes, or away from the sex scenes."

"Isn't there a term for those scenes?"

"Yeah. I call them irrelevant."

"I thought they were referred to as 'redeeming social value' scenes."

"Yeah, that too. Some people like that stuff. Or maybe they need it for a breather before I get them excited again."

"Oh. Your scenes excite people?"

"Well, sure. Don't they excite you?"

"I'm not seeking my testimony. You agree that your scenes arouse people sexually?"

"I hope so. They arouse me."

"And when someone is aroused, what happens?"

"That depends, I guess. On the person and on the circs."

"For instance?"

"Well, there's some that like to get aroused and sort of stay that way. Others want to do something about it."

"And what would you say they do?"

"That depends again. If there's someone handy to go to bed with—like, maybe they're married or something."

"And if someone isn't handy?"

"I guess some of them masturbate."

"Or go out and commit a sex crime?"

"I doubt it. When a guy—I suppose you're mostly talking about guys now—gets that worked up, he's in no mood to find a stranger and go through the whole business of a crime. That would turn off a normal guy. He'd have to be sick."

"But you know that sex crimes are committed. There are sex criminals."

"Yes. Like people who don't read about it, or see shows about it, brooders. Or people with queer hang-ups. Like for instance s.m." He glanced up at the judge. "Sadomasochism . . ." She nodded gravely and he continued, "But most of the time I'd say they're committed by people without an outlet."

"What's an outlet?"

"A handy sexual partner. An erotic book. Like mine."

Lew stared at the ceiling for some minutes. "Of course, Mr. Jorgenson, you are not a psychologist or psychiatrist, so you wouldn't know—"

"Sure I would. There was this study that a famous writer made a couple of years back. He asked this psychoanalyst and—"

Lahey broke in, "I don't think we need—"

Marc was on his feet. "I think we do, Your Honor. If the

prosecutor won't allow the answer, we'll ask the same question on cross-examination."

Lahey said, "Oh, go ahead," and walked away from Jorgenson, who went on, "This writer asked a psychoanalyst and a psychologist if showing or describing a sex act, in a book or in a movie, could make anyone commit sex crimes. They sent out questionnaires to psychiatrists and psychologists all over the country and got back more than three thousand answers. I think it was eighty percent who said there was no connection between reading porn and committing violent acts. I know. I memorized that writer's piece about it."

Lew Lahey waved a dismissing hand at this testimony. "Now, if we can get back to the issue. These redeeming-social-value scenes that you say you don't write. Who does?"

"Someone else."

"So I assumed. Can you name such a person?"

"Sure. She said I could." He nodded to Judy among the spectators. "Judy Cuneo."

"Are you eager to have her write these scenes?"

"I don't mind."

"Did you and your publisher, Mr. Snaith, ever discuss these scenes?"

"What's in them, you mean? No."

"I mean, did you discuss the business of having them written and added to your manuscript?"

"Sure."

"What was said about them—about a reason for their being added?"

"They rounded the novels. And also, the law likes them there."

"Wasn't what the law likes the main reason for their being written?"

"It was a reason."

"Without those scenes, your books would have been subject to legal action? They could have been banned?"

"I don't know. I'm not a lawyer. Anyhow, there's a lot of

erotic books with about as much sex in them as any of mine and with about the same amount of non-sex stuff."

"But those books—the sex scenes and the non-sex scenes were all written by the same person?"

"Most of the time—I guess so."

"That *does* make a difference, doesn't it?"

"I don't see how. Suppose only one author writes a book and it has both kind of scenes. Who's to say whether the author put the non-sex in to make it better, or to get it within the law?"

"But," said Lew, "you must admit they'd know that whatever the reason, it came from a single mind. Not two or more conspiring."

Judge Negley glanced quizzically at the defense table. But neither Marc nor Jay seemed inclined to interrupt Lahey's argumentative questioning.

"What's wrong with collaboration? Do Masters and Johnson conspire? Suppose one described the clinic and that machine they use and the other one described the patients and their problems. Would that make their books dirty?"

Lew said, "I'm allowing you to ask me questions because they really form part of your answers. Masters and Johnson are scientists."

"Okay," said Jorgenson. "So they aren't artists. They still got rights."

Lew went back to his table. Over his shoulder he said, "He's all yours."

Jay glanced at Marc, who rose and walked toward the stand. "Mr. Jorgenson, how many books have you had published in Solus editions?"

"Six."

"How have they sold?"

"Not very well, I guess."

"Don't you know? Don't you get royalty statements?"

"No. I write them for a flat fee."

"That's not the usual author-publisher arrangement, is it?"

"It is in the paperback erotica field."

"Why should that be?"

"Because the retail price of the books is low. And they don't sell many copies. Not like paperback reprints of books that were hardcover best sellers. If I got a few cents' royalty on every copy of my books and they sold, say, ten or twenty thousand—and they don't—that might be maybe a thousand dollars. It wouldn't pay me."

"How much do you get?"

"Fifteen hundred a book. That doesn't really pay me either, but for maybe a few weeks' work, I do it."

"How do you know your books sell twenty thousand or fewer?"

"That's what Mr. Snaith says. Hard-core doesn't sell; other publishers say so, too. There aren't many bookstores that sell them. And there isn't a big market for them. There's so much frank sex in some of the big best sellers that almost nobody buys my kind of book any more. It isn't like the old days."

"What old days?"

"Back before I was writing. Back in the early fifties and for years before. There wasn't any Supreme Court decision blocking the censors then. So everything got censored, even things like *Lady Chatterly's Lover* and *Fanny Hill.* They even banned the Kinsey Reports from Army P.X.'s."

"But how did that condition affect books like yours?"

"Hah! Back then, little paperbacks like mine sold under the counter for anything from five to ten dollars a copy. They were forbidden. A porn publisher could make real dough then; so could a porn writer."

"Do you think those times will ever return?"

"If there's book banning—sure."

Lew Lahey was on his feet.

Marc asked quickly, "Mr. Jorgenson, we rehearsed this last testimony, didn't we?"

"Sure."

"Is your prediction nevertheless your honest opinion?"

Jorgenson spread his hands. "Well, of course. Look at Prohibition—"

Lahey practically shouted. "Your Honor! This is, by the defense's own admission, staged. It's also irrelevant and incompetent and nothing but the witness's conclusion."

"I agree," said Judge Negley. "Sustained."

Marc said to Jorgenson, "That's all." He picked up a sheaf of papers and turned toward the bench. "At this time we submit financial records of certain publishers proving that the sales of so-called pornography have been declining and that such lines as Solus Books earned more before *Roth v. U.S.* than they do today."

Lahey said, "I object to this characterization of testimony by the defense."

"And I'd sustain you if a jury were present."

"Again, Your Honor," said Marc, "We're merely trying to save time."

Jorgenson had left the stand. Now Lahey suddenly said, "Mr. Jorgenson, there's another question or two I'd like to ask."

Jorgenson looked from Lahey to Marc. Judge Negley said, "The witness will please take the stand again. You're still under oath."

Jorgenson climbed into the chair and Lahey said, "You say you write one of your books in a few weeks. How many?"

"About four. No more than that."

"And get fifteen hundred dollars for it? How many do you do a year?"

"Three last year. Two so far this one."

"So from these books you earn forty-five hundred dollars for a quarter of a year's work. That's not bad, added to your income from your other writing, is it?"

"It's pretty good, for my kind of novel."

"Ah, yes. And just how, when you're thinking about it privately, do you characterize your kind of novel, Mr. Jorgenson?"

Jorgenson didn't hesitate. "Autobiographical," he said.

26

At four, Judge Negley adjourned until the following morning. Before that, Lahey had called Judy Cuneo, who testified that she had added material to Jorgenson manuscripts, that such material had been intended to afford breaks between sex scenes and that, yes, it was also intended to give the stories social value, that much of this insert material consisted of relevant quotes from classic prose and appropriate public-domain poetry. She expressed no interest in what she inserted or in the material Jorgenson wrote. To one question concerning the people who read Solus books she confessed her inability to understand their motives. "Why read about it?" she wondered. "It's more fun to do it."

The defense had no questions. Lahey then offered *Ecstatic Excursions* in evidence, admitted that it was improper to cite particular passages, but made it clear that the prosecution was asking a permanent injunction on the grounds of its inclusion of *Miss Baker's Dozen*. The judge accepted the evidence, which she already held and had read over the weekend, and recessed court until ten the following morning.

Snaith took Hester, Jay and Paul De Witt along with his own party of Jorgenson, Judy, Marc and Laura to dinner at an inn on the line between Guernsey and Morris counties. And there they encountered the first hint of the resentment which would grow and take unexpected forms.

They were enjoying their drinks at table and listening to Paul recount the inn's history. It seemed that it had been established in pre-Revolutionary days by a devotee of musketry who called it The Ball and Ramrod. In 1814, perhaps in empathy with the White House, all but its hearth, fireplace and massive chimney had burned down. In the 1830's a new structure had been built around the remnants and opened as The Channel Isle, which—through several restorations and enlargements—had remained its official name to the present day. Meanwhile, as local high schoolers with an ear for history's esoteria learned of its original designation they took to calling it Ball and Ramrod with a surreptitiousness which, over the years and the mores, became increasingly open, casual and nowadays the vernacular term of all but the most staid local residents.

"Hello." They looked up as Paul was finishing to see the girl with the long red hair standing behind Hester.

"Hello, Annie," said Jay and introduced Mansfield's star reporter to the company.

"How's the trial going?" she asked Jay.

"What do you think? You were there."

"Yes, but I'd like it from your viewpoint."

Jay shrugged. "We're confident. If that's any good to you. You won't be out for three more days, and by that time we may have a ruling. And nothing said now will be news."

Annie looked down at Hester. "Will this experience alter your policy any way in the library?"

"Now, Annie. You know better than that. Nothing could make me—OW!" She gasped. "All right. Here's a hot story for you. My lawyer just kicked me under the table. Do you think he's trying to tell me something?"

"It's a cinch nobody's telling me anything. See you." And Annie turned away.

At this point, as Snaith was asking who wanted seconds, they were interrupted by a florid man in a loud and tightly buttoned sports jacket. He had crossed to them from the bar, where he obviously had consumed seconds if not thirds or possibly, in either sense, fifths.

He stood weaving slightly a few feet from Hester and

vaguely pointed a finger at her. "It's bad enough you putting . . . putting"—he seemed to search for a word—"smut in the libr'ry. But why"—he waved to the rest at table—"di'ja have to bring New York riffraff int' th' town? Huh? Why?"

The manager, or maybe maître d', who had greeted and seated them, hastened up behind the florid one. "All right, now, Mr. Hayley. Let's not have any trouble." And he tried to lead him away.

The man planted his feet more firmly. "I'm not makin' trouble. She's makin' trouble. They're all"—he waved again at the table—"makin' trouble. Comin' to town an' . . . an' disturbin' the peace."

A diner at a nearby table quietly pushed back his chair, rose, and as gently as possible, took Mr. Hayley's arm. Together with the manager he soothed him out of the dining room, presently returning alone. "Sorry about that," he said to the group in general. Jay and Paul seemed to know him, acknowledged the apology and thanked him for his intervention. Then Paul introduced him as a Mr. Goodwin. Goodwin nodded to the others, started toward his own table, and hesitated. "Of course," he said, "Hayley's tight. And certainly you're all welcome here in Mansfield. But that doesn't mean I like dirty books any more than Hayley does." He regarded Paul. "I shouldn't have thought you did, either."

"And what," asked Paul, "makes you think I do?"

"I'd heard you were appearing for the defense."

"True," said Paul.

"Well, then?"

"That doesn't mean I like dirty books. And, quite incidentally, I'm not accepting that characterization of the work in question. However, even if it were, I'd still appear."

Goodwin waved a dismissing hand. "Oh, I know, I know. You're on a new civil-liberties kick."

"You could say so," said Paul. "That's what we're defending. One of your civil liberties."

"*Mine?* I don't want to read the damn book!"

"Quite. And that's what we're defending."

"Hah!" exclaimed Goodwin. "Another one of your academic jokes!"

"Not a bit academic. If this county—or state, or nation—could forbid the reading of something, then it could compel the reading of something else. The two actions are quite similar. Some think they're connected by a thing called fascism."

"You must be kidding," said Goodwin.

"Not at all," Paul answered. "The freedom to read is inextricably entwined with the freedom not to read."

Goodwin shook his head chidingly. Then, chuckling at the foolish witticisms of the elderly scholar, he went back to his table.

Jay said, "Neatly put. Of course, you're lucky Goodwin isn't a lawyer."

Paul looked at him inquiringly. "And if he were?"

"He'd no doubt have asked you if you consider the school system fascistic. Or do you think children have the right not to read?"

"No," said Paul, "not while they're learning the art. And not while they're being sufficiently exposed to literature. That maturity gained, I think they have as much right not to read as a man, having learned something about religion, has the right to embrace any creed he wishes, or atheism."

"That's all very well," said Hester, "but meanwhile we librarians are up against the old demand to 'Keep that book off your shelves' because a child, even a teen-ager, might get hold of it."

Paul smiled at her. "Actually, all you're required to do is keep so-called adult books where children don't browse unsupervised." Paul leaned forward, cupping his highball glass. "For my own part, I wouldn't shut the kids away from any books. I don't think they'd have the interest to read them until they had the modicum of maturity to understand them. By that time, I doubt the dangers of their blandishments."

"That," said Laura, "is what Jenny Hayes said the other night."

Paul laughed. "I'll bet her husband didn't entirely agree with her."

"He didn't," said Marc. "Rupert takes a liberal but not entirely permissive view."

"It isn't a bad view," said Paul, "just a bit limited from where I stand. But then, where I stand is, ideologically, in the heart of Copenhagen."

It wasn't a crash as much as a series of short, snapping sounds followed by a heavy bump and muffled exclamations.

Paul, awakened in his ground-floor bedroom, was sure that it had come from very nearly above him—from the master bedroom belonging to his absent daughter and son-in-law or a guest room directly next to it. He looked at his bedside clock. Almost two. They'd turned in shortly before one. He heard doors opening above and what sounded like startled whispers. Pushing out of bed, he struggled into his bathrobe and went out into the lower hall. From the foot of the stairs he could see that lights were on in the upper hall. And someone was talking. In worried tones. He climbed the stairs slowly. Hester in a mannish dressing gown and Jay in rumpled pajamas were listening to a fully dressed Marc and Laura, who were standing in the doorway of a guest room. When Marc saw Paul, he strode toward him. Farther down the hall, Judy and Snaith were peering from separate doorways.

"Look, I'm frightfully sorry," Marc said. "I'm afraid I've done some serious damage."

He led Paul toward the guest room, and Laura, stepping aside to let them in, said, "It was my fault."

Marc pointed to the antique bed. The spread still covered it but showed deep rumples across its middle. The ancient bed frame sagged, and beneath, where the spread was rumpled most, touched the floor.

"It's badly cracked," said Marc. "Underneath—the slats seem broken. I fell across it."

"Marc! I—I tripped you." Laura turned to Paul. "*We* fell across it."

Marc, on his knees, peering under the bed, said, "I was forcing myself on her. She very properly resisted."

"I'm not sure I wanted to," said Laura.

"Exactly," said Marc, "that's why it was my fault we fell."

"I mean," said Laura, "I'm not sure I wanted to resist."

Paul had crouched next to Marc. Now both of them looked up, Marc more swiftly than Paul. But Laura had slipped from the room. Marc started to rise as though to follow her, but Hester, in the doorway and glancing down the hall, motioned him to stay where he was. The room had been lit by the bedlamp only. Now Hester, as if momentarily to change the mood, snapped the wall switch and several other lamps came on.

Marc slowly returned to his knees and to his concern about the bed. "There," he said to Paul, "you can see the ends of slats on the floor. The frame is cracked."

Paul said, "I'm sure it can be fixed. At any rate, there's nothing we can do tonight. I'll have it looked at later on. Whoever was using this room can move to one of the children's. There are couches in each of them."

Hester said, "This was Laura's. I'll tell her." And she turned away.

Marc said to Paul, "I'm afraid no repair will help much. But at least let me know what it comes to. I want to pay." He was still on his knees, looking under the bed.

"It's not that important," said Paul. "And I consider it my fault, actually. Anyone who owns so old a bed should confine it to the elderly, the infirm and the passionless."

"When you put Laura in here," Marc mumbled, "you were assigning it to the innocent. You couldn't figure that I would louse things up."

Paul squatted next to him. "You must have injured your head when you fell. That girl has just made the most vital admission of her young life. That's important—next to a bed. If you know what I don't mean."

Marc didn't answer him. In the now-greater illumination, he had seen something under the broken bed. He carefully reached in and gently lifted a dark oblong out of the shadows. He swiveled around until he was sitting on the floor, holding the little object in his hands. He blew on it gently and heavy dust stirred.

"What is it?" Paul asked.

"Some kind of a book"—Marc turned it over—"in a slipcase. It must have been inside the slats. It's covered with dust."

Paul, leaning across Marc's shoulder, peered closely at the thing and Marc offered it to him. Paul, taking it, turned it slowly in his hands, blowing at it some more and trying to get additional light on it. He struggled to his feet and carried it over to a table lamp. He turned the case again, looking closely not only at its front and back but also at its ends. Except for grime, it was unmarked. Not even its open end, revealing the book's spine, showed any printing or engraving.

With infinite care, Paul worked the book from its case and put both on the table. Taking a kerchief from his robe, he gently dusted at the book's cover. "It's certainly leather, and very old." He put a finger under the cover's overhang and raised it until the book was open. "It's still firmly hinged."

The revealed first sheet, a flyleaf, was heavy, vellumlike, yellowed—and blank. He carefully turned that, too. Under it was the first page of what appeared to be a blankbook of good quality, lined paper, now yellow and fragile to the touch.

"There's writing here." Paul bent closely over some barely discernible script. Then he crossed to the bed table, pulled open its drawer and returned with a flashlight. He trained the beam on the faded script, trying various angles to gain illumination and reduce glare. "It's a name," he said. "Abigail something."

"Not Adams, I suppose."

"No. This is a lot rounder than her handwriting. Hers was sharply slanted with curved ascenders." Paul looked up at Marc and there was excitement in his voice. "But the ink and paper look old enough for her." He bent over the book again. "The surname starts with an *L—L* and then an *a—*an *aw—Law*. Then there's an *r—rans. Lawrans—*Abigail Lawrans." He blew air thoughtfully between his teeth.

"Ever hear the name?"

Paul shook his head. "N-o-o. Not spelled that way exactly." He bent to the page again. "There's a date. Here—under the name. Can you make it out?"

Marc's hair touched the side of Paul's grizzled crewcut. "I think it's 17—1777. And isn't that a dash after it?"

"That's what I thought," said Paul. "And nothing after the dash. No end date."

"You mean as though someone started whatever it is—and didn't finish?"

"Maybe." Paul turned a page and wrinkled his eyes at it. "Yes. I think so. This starts up here near the top." He pointed to the upper left-hand corner of the right-hand page. "It's a date—April fourteenth, I think." He bent as close to it as he could, then moved his head away. "I think it starts 'This day' —it's almost certainly a diary, a journal. Something begun, or pretending to begin, in April 1777."

"And never finished?" Marc asked. "Because there's no other date after the dash?"

"Maybe." Paul straightened and put his hands on his

cramped lower back. "I'd like to take this down to my study. I've a pretty good magnifying glass there. I wouldn't sleep much more tonight without trying to learn what this is. Care to come along?"

Marc's eyes went automatically to the door and the hall beyond. He hesitated.

Paul continued rapidly, "It won't be easy for both of us to examine it together . . ."

"I know," said Marc. "You take it, by all means. You're the expert on this sort of thing. I wouldn't know what I was looking at. Anyhow, it's yours."

Paul weighed it in his hands. "Is it?"

"Of course. It was hidden in your bed."

"Does that make it mine?"

"Whose else?"

"I wonder. Still, you're the expert there—on property." He laughed. "I'm certainly jumping the gun. This may be worthless. Maybe someone's prank on the poor old historian."

Marc watched Paul disappear down the stairs. Then he looked along the empty hall. One of the bedroom doors was partly open and a narrow path of light flowed from it.

"What time is it?"

"Almost four-thirty. I thought you were asleep."

"Umm. I was. You know what?"

"What?"

"I don't think Jorgenson writes this kind of thing so well, after all."

"Nobody does. Not as good as it is. Would you rather he didn't try?"

"N-o-o. It's okay. For those who like it spelled out."

"Or don't know all about it—its variations."

"Like me? I don't, do I?"

"Not yet."

"You know what I want to be?"

"What?"

"A slow study. Nice and slow."

"It can take years."

"Umm. . . ." She silently savored the thought. Then: "Marc."

"Yes?"

"I've made up my mind about something. After listening in court today—and now, after this—I want you to put me on the stand tomorrow."

"*Now!* Not a chance."

"Why not, for heaven's sake?"

"I'm not doing anything to make your mother angrier."

"I thought we just were."

"This she needn't find out about. Unless you want to tell her. But putting you on the stand would probably make the papers. It was a dumb idea from the start."

"Why? My testimony might help."

"It isn't worth it. We'll probably win without it."

"Mother couldn't be more down on us than she is right now. And I want to help. Anyhow, who knows she's my mother? I mean, around here. How could it get in the papers? Hester won't say anything. And you don't need to ask me about my family on the stand, do you?"

"Lord, no. But, Laura, this would really cut the cord."

"No. Mother cut the cord. If anyone's making a public spectacle, it's Mother. I'm defending my friends against a vicious charge."

"If you get on that stand, won't Apsemont recognize you?"

"I don't think so. I was in the audience at the A.C.E. convention the only time I saw him. We were introduced afterwards, but that was about three years ago. He wouldn't remember. If he learns I'm from downstate Ohio he might connect my name . . . but I don't care. Mother can't touch me. Not now."

He reached sleepily toward her. "That goes for everyone else outside this room."

29

As they came down to breakfast, they found a note from Paul on the dining room table.

Friends: I'll see you later in the morning—perhaps about eleven—in court. I trust I won't be needed on the stand before that.

I'm off to Princeton to see a friend about something that turned up last night. Perhaps we can lunch together. I may have a matter of interest to impart. P. D. W.

The courtroom was even sultrier than it had been the day before. When Judge Negley called them to order, Marc summoned Laura as his first witness. She gave her name and her Barbizon address, and Marc quickly led her through an establishment of her employment by Tabard and her duties as switchboard operator and general assistant.

"Do you perform other services there?"

"I write material for Solus books. As Miss Cuneo did."

Apsemont, at the prosecution's table, was watching her with a puzzled expression. Meanwhile Lew Lahey had risen.

"Your Honor, the witness indicated that she's only recently joined Tabard Press. *Miss Baker's Dozen* was published two years ago."

"Your Honor," said Marc, "Miss Conroy is here as a worker in a unique field—the same one Miss Cuneo worked in. Therefore she's something of an expert witness."

"If you can so establish her . . ." Judge Negley said.

Marc turned back to Laura. "Miss Conroy, what is your background as a writer?"

"I've written essays and short stories. I've edited the literary magazine at Damascus College. I've been writing for Tabard Press for long enough to know—"

With a patronizing smile, Lew Lahey started to his feet again, but Apsemont pulled him back and whispered to him. Judge Negley waited impatiently. Again Lew Lahey rose. "We have no objection at this time."

The judge looked at him quizzically. "The point of irrelevance might well be taken."

"I'll waive it," said Lahey. "We'll accept Miss Conroy as an expert."

"Really?" said Judge Negley. "She must have become expert pretty fast."

"Yes," said Marc dryly. "May I proceed?"

The judge nodded, rather wearily, and Marc turned to Laura. "Miss Conroy, do you write pornography?"

"No."

"Do you write material for books which you consider pornographic?"

"No."

"How would you describe Ralph Jorgenson's material?"

"As unrelieved erotica."

"Unrelieved?"

"Yes. It's my job to break up the monotony."

"Miss Cuneo told us that she injected passages from the classics and relevant statistics into the books she worked on. Is that what you do?"

"No. I write original material."

"Have you read much erotica?"

"Quite a bit lately. I wanted to become familiar with—with the genre."

"Have you studied the art of literary criticism?"

"Yes."

"Without classifying yourself as a literary critic, do you consider yourself as well trained in that area?"

"As a student, yes. At least, I guess my teachers thought so. I graduated magna. And my major was literature."

"What makes the Jorgenson material erotica rather than pornography—indeed, hard-core pornography?"

"The quality of his writing. It has genuine literary merit, in my opinion. He writes with poetic images, and then counterpoints with abrupt hard-edged realism."

"Do you consider literary merit as having social value?"

"Yes. As good music, or good painting."

"Have you ever encountered pornography which you consider lacking in social value?"

"Yes. On the walls of lavatories, for instance."

"Does the Jorgenson material include words that you have seen on such walls?"

"Certainly. But he uses the words in context, in interesting narrative—and with good writing."

"What effect does Jorgenson's material, or other writing like it, have on you?"

"It depends on the story—or the scene. Sometimes it's terrifying. Often it's amusing. Or, it can be titillating."

"And when it's titillating, do you consider it deleterious?"

"No. It makes me feel alive. In what I've recently come to know is a very healthy way."

"Thank you," said Marc. "Thank you very much." Over his shoulder he said, "Your witness."

Lahey walked briskly toward the stand. "Miss Conroy. You gave your address as that of a hotel in New York. Is that your permanent residence?"

"Yes. Not the hotel. But New York is."

"Is it your legal residence?"

"New York will be."

"Where had it been?"

"In Ohio."

"Near your college? Damascus I think you said. That's in the southern part of the state, isn't it?"

"Yes."

"And your town—your legal residence there—was . . .?"

"Ludgrove."

"I believe that's near Cincinnati?"

"Yes."

"And Ludgrove, I understand, is the home of Mrs. Jessica Conroy. Are you related to her?"

"I'm her daughter."

"Your mother is the head of Americans for Clean Entertainment, isn't she?"

"Yes. She founded it."

"And that organization brought this complaint through its representatives here, Miss and Mr. Apsemont."

"So I understand."

"Do you feel loyalty to your mother?"

"Objection!" Marc shouted. "The question is irrelevant."

"We are trying, Your Honor," said Lahey, "to determine whether the witness is testifying out of some—some tension between herself and her mother."

Judge Negley considered momentarily. "I'll allow it." She nodded to Laura.

"Yes," said Laura. "I feel loyalty to my mother up to a point."

"Up to what point?" asked Lahey.

"Up to the point where I consider a complaint of hers unjustified."

"What do you think your mother's attitude to your appearance here would be?"

"She wouldn't like it."

"But that hasn't deterred you?"

"No. I'm more concerned with—with justice."

"Oh. Very noble, I'm sure. Does your mother know that you are employed by Tabard?"

"Yes. I told her."

"And did you tell her you were—how did you put it—breaking the monotony of Solus books?"

"No."

"You withheld that information from her. Why?"

"It would have upset her. I don't want to do that."

"Living in New York is expensive. Are you getting an allowance from home?"

"Yes—I was."

"Isn't that why you concealed the nature of your work?"

"Not really. Since I got the job I'm self-sufficient."

"New York hotels aren't cheap."

"I know. I've been looking . . ." Her voice gained volume and assurance. "I expect to move. Almost immediately."

Lahey walked away. Judge Negley asked, "Redirect?"

Marc came to his feet. "Thank you, Your Honor. I've heard everything I want to."

30

During Laura's cross-examination, Paul had entered and taken one of the few empty seats—next to Anne Semple Cobb. Jay, turning, nodded to him, which caused Marc to look around. Paul raised his bushy eyebrows, pursed his lips and slightly rocked his head as might a bearer of surprising news.

Jay called a Madelaine Goldsmith to the stand, established her as a resident of Mansfield, a member of the faculty of Douglas College and the bearer of a doctorate in sociology. Skillfully questioned by Jay, she described the varieties of Mansfield's social groups, estimated their various attitudes toward sex (based on her observations of pressures on the Board of Education, objections to and support for certain recently exhibited motion pictures), cited divorce, unwed motherhood and similar statistics, reported the growing liberalism of sermon topics, the acceptance of sex education, enumerated the forces in town backing a state abortion bill, and testified to her professional observation of changes in book-buying patterns at paperback stands, the small local book and stationery store and the borrowing patterns at the public library. She then testified to having read *Miss Baker's Dozen* and expressed her opinion that it was not obscene in terms of the contemporary standards of the community.

Lahey, cross-examining, made the mistake of asking whether it wasn't true that she had read the work in question only after being requested to testify for the defense. No, that was when she'd reread it. She'd read it originally, as had a number of her fellow faculty members, in the course of an informal study of Douglas students' reading habits which seemed to be improving (Objection! Irrelevant! Unresponsive! Overruled—the answer seems cogent to the issue)—improving the general interest in reading of all kinds.

With this self-inflicted wound Lahey sat, and Marc, turning to signal Paul that he was on next, saw him in earnest conversation with the red-headed Annie.

When Marc began to establish Paul's expertise, Lahey offered to stipulate his qualifications as historian, literary critic and perceptive observer of human behavior in general and Mansfield's in particular. But for the record, Marc led him through a modestly stated but impressive recital of his academic positions, his published works, the Societies here and abroad before which he'd read papers, and his degrees—both those earned and those conferred to honor him. In his direct examination Marc took—and Lahey did not challenge—wide latitude. He went from *Miss Baker's Dozen* to other works in *Ecstatic Excursions,* in particular *Jurgen.*

"When was *Jurgen* published?"

"I believe it was in 1919."

"How was it received?"

"Variously."

Marc waited and Paul went on, "Its reception by the critics was somewhat different from that by the public. And entirely different from that by the puritanical."

"Could you tell us about each?"

"Yes. Briefly, the leading critical journals acclaimed it. The *New York Times Book Review* admired its philosophy, its humor, its whimsicality. The Chicago *Tribune,* as was mentioned yesterday, placed its author above all his contemporaries. As was pointed out here, that reviewer neglected Joyce among others. I would add that he also wasn't afraid of Virginia Woolf. I've looked up these reviews—in *Book Review Digest*—since the book was attacked last week."

Paul crossed his legs into a more comfortable position. "As for the public, it ignored *Jurgen.* That is, it ignored it until—"

He reached into a side pocket of his jacket and took out a rumpled sheet of notepaper bearing a few typed lines. "I found this short statement in Anne Lyon Haight's *Banned Books*—the third edition, published in 1970 by R. R. Bowker Company." Paul held the paper up to the light and read: " '1920. United States. *Jurgen* was prosecuted by the New York Society for the Suppression of Vice. Several hundred people prominent in public and literary life presented petitions protesting against this action. This publicity established a hitherto obscure novel as a best seller.' " He shoved the paper back into his pocket.

"Then," Marc said, "an attempt to censor made a worthy book popular?"

"Yes. In that instance. In many others, it merely increases the distribution, openly or covertly, of much unworthy expression. That's why I believe the effects of censorship to be worse than the effects of license."

"You have explored that theme in some of your writings?"

"I have. Those essays are now collected in *The Perils of Orthodoxy.*"

"What did you intend to convey with that title?"

"That the less democratic a society is, the less tolerant it becomes. All orthodoxies, whether they be religious or political, imperil expression. Censorship was a bulwark of Nazism, and still is of Communism and fascism."

"In your opinion, can *Miss Baker's Dozen* harm this community?"

"Yes. By being banned. Once banned, it would become notorious, its popularity would increase and spread. As a result, imitations of it—inevitably vulgar and unworthy—would be written, published and sold like Prohibition rotgut. Instead of being sold through legitimate bookstores and made available in libraries, such books would be pushed not only to adults but also to children who, without the notoriety, wouldn't have heard of them—or hearing of them, found them attractive."

"Perhaps I can save Mr. Lahey a question. You do, then,

consider *Miss Baker's Dozen* to be a somewhat vulgar novel?"

"Of course I do. Well written and somewhat vulgar. It belongs to what is sometimes termed soft-core pornography."

"But you don't object to it?"

"Of course not. I'd hate to see it become anyone's steady, let alone sole, literary diet. Just as I'd deplore newspaper reading that included nothing but the gossip columns and the comic strips. Or TV viewing that confined itself to soap operas, violence or the average run of situation comedies. But that doesn't mean I'd ban the comic strip or the soap opera. Why should I? I can look at what I want to or turn the set off. I can read the parts of the paper I choose, or discard it. If my neighbor chooses a different reading and viewing course, then each of us has an available liberty. He has the liberty to pursue his enjoyment. I have the liberty to deplore it."

"You referred to *Miss Baker's Dozen* as 'soft-core' pornography. What about hard-core? How would you define it? And would you control it?"

"I understand hard-core to be a monotonous—I thank Miss Conroy for the word—succession of sexual, often sadomasochistic, sometimes scatological episodes, reported without art or any variety except on the most trivial level of who, what, where." Paul paused. "As for how I'd control it . . . I'd let it die the natural death it is approaching. In 1970 the *Report of the Commission on Obscenity and Pornography* revealed that the total sale of hard-core (almost entirely in paperback) represented less than one and a quarter percent of the mass-market paperback sales in the United States. Add to the mass-market paperbacks all scholarly and other paperbacks and all the hardcover books published here, and the percentage of hard-core drops to an infinitesimal part of one percent of all new books. Ask any publisher or experienced bookseller and you'll learn that hard-core books have been dying. What the publisher of hard-core desperately needs is a new Prohibition era affecting his books. Then, instead of selling them from a few under-the-counter stores, he could sell them, at far higher prices, to a suddenly large and avid public. Avid for the forbidden."

There was no cross-examination. Jay rested and Judge Negley promised a ruling the following morning. Jorgenson and Judy went back to New York, he to his typewriter, she to her baby. Snaith decided to stay over for the decision, as did Marc. Somehow it was taken for granted that Laura would stay, too. They were still in the courtroom when Paul said, "I have something I'd like to tell you. I think it may involve law, publishing, genealogies. Anyhow, where could we eat quietly —not in a public restaurant?"

"In the library," said Hester. "We could send out for sandwiches. And we've genealogies there, if local ones will do."

"I think they're the only ones that will," Paul said.

31

Paul had tossed his coat and his knitted tie on a shelf, straddled a chair, and with his arms folded across its back, looked around at the rest of them lounging in Hester's office. Her assistants were out behind the counter and she'd indicated that she and her guests didn't want to be disturbed. Her assistants understood this. After all, Hester was on trial as well as the book and here she was with her lawyers, the publisher and that attractive girl who a visitor to the library said had been identified in court as co-author of books like the one under indictment. And, of course, Paul De Witt, whose membership on the Library Board was only one of the reasons he should be in conference with Hester.

Paul launched at once into his story.

"Last night Marc Holland found an old book in my home. I hadn't known it was there. Indeed, it was concealed. In an antique. We examined it and it appeared to be a personal journal apparently written by a woman named Abigail Lawrans. That's L-a-w-r-a-n-s." He paused.

Nobody spoke.

"It bore a date. 1777."

"Is that why you wanted genealogies?" Hester began to rise.

"Yes. But let's wait a bit. Later last night I used a strong light and a pretty powerful magnifying glass and satisfied myself that it was written in a style which seemed to conform to the date on it. I managed with a little difficulty to read various passages, a few of which I copied and have here. I'll read them to you presently. If this journal is genuine, then its content is sensational. This morning I drove over to Princeton, where Professor Harry Chayne is conducting a summer graduate seminar in his field. Some of you may know that his specialty is American history and, in particular, its documents and their characteristics. I've left the journal with him because he wants to subject it to various laboratory tests. Meanwhile he is strongly inclined to believe that it could be two centuries old, that not only the ink and paper—subject to his tests—seem that old but the very handwriting is typical of a reasonably educated person of the late eighteenth century. He is unfamiliar, as I am, with the name Lawrans—spelled that way—and certainly with anyone of precisely that name living then or now in this area. Yet the text—as much as we examined—makes many references to this part of New Jersey, to Morristown, Pompton, Brunswick and other places in the immediate vicinity, and it also has references to various families who are known to have lived in these parts in the Colonial and Revolutionary periods."

He pushed off his chair and went to his jacket, returning with several sheets of large notepaper. "Let me read you the opening passage in this journal. In typical diary style, it leads off with a date—April fourteenth."

He began to read slowly and expressively. The use of capital letters and the various misspellings (by today's standards) became evident to them later when they examined his copied notes.

"*April 14.* This day at last there is such promise of Spring that my Spirits are renued and I have determined to keep the Journal so long contemplated. In these pages I pledge to find that Honesty of expression which otherwise eludes me. But should I find myself incapable of retailing in these Secret Writings the truth of my Life, I shall destroy this Volume and all I may have written herein. Had I not fortuitously come upon a Place of Concealment for this Journal I would ne'er have begun it for fear of spying eyes."

Paul looked around at them. "Chayne was able to find in two published local diaries confirmation that early April of 1777 had been cold, rainy and gloomy. In the middle of that month, the weather turned suddenly pleasant. I might add that if Abigail's place of concealment was within the close-set slats of the bed from which it finally fell, she had reason to trust her hiding place."

"This is fascinating," said Lincoln Snaith, "but actually, aren't there many such personal records of that period?"

"Indeed there are. But I had reason to use the word 'sensational' before. Let me read you a shorter passage from a bit farther on:

"*May 19.* Until last night I had not seen him since our meeting in the third week of April. He was ardent to a measure that I could attribute to nothing so much as the length of our separation. I know that his Wife and her Ladies are with him now at his Headquarters and this Knowledge made me treasure all the more the Night he stole for me."

Paul looked up. Into a puzzled, almost stunned group.

"Paul," said Jay finally, "in 1777—did anyone else have his headquarters around here?"

"No one else whose wife and entourage visited him that spring."

"And *his* wife and ladies did visit him just at that time?"

Paul nodded very slowly. "For weeks. From April on—after he'd become ill in March of that year."

"Jesus Christ!" Jay almost shouted. "She *has* to be talking about Washington!"

Paul said nothing.

Hester, without moving from her chair, seemed to be seizing his lapels. "Paul! You'd know. Do you believe this?"

"Let's not," said Paul, "get *too* excited. I said 'sensational.' I didn't say 'proven.' "

"But what," insisted Hester, "do you think?"

"At this point, pending more from Chayne, I'd *guess* the lady wrote it. And did so in 1777 when Washington's headquarters were in Morristown or nearby from the beginning of the year off and on into September. And"—Paul spread his hand holding the notes—"it's well documented that Martha and several of her ladies were with him part of the time."

"But has there ever been a whisper of scandal about him?" Marc asked. "He wasn't supposed to drink, or swear, or anything."

"Some of that is legend," said Paul. "We have military memoirs which make it clear that at least on the battlefield or in camp, he could summon a necessary round oath. Nor was he entirely abstemious. He was, however, very moderate for his day. As for 'anything,' I've never read or heard of any suggestion that he was ever unfaithful to Martha."

"How old was he then—in 1777?" asked Hester.

"Forty-five."

"And how long had he been married?"

"Eighteen years."

"Hmmph!" said Hester.

"The eighteen-year itch?" asked Jay.

Laura frowned. Marc shook his head with exaggerated disbelief.

"Let's remember," said Paul, "that even if this journal is genuine, its contents need not be true."

"Why?" asked Snaith. "She never let anyone see it. Who could she have been kidding?"

"Herself, perhaps," Paul said. "She might have been an unhappy spinster creating a secret fantasy life."

"Is there more about Washington?" asked Snaith.

"She never mentions his name. But just skimming it—that's all I had time to do—I encountered references to her attending large local assemblies at his headquarters and several other pretty explicit references to nights—but let me read you two other passages:

"*June 24.* I can no longer tease myself that I am not two months with Child. Nor can I even speculate that it is not Ours, there having been none other in my life since Camden on the very eve of the Declaration."

"My God!" said Snaith. "This is dynamite!"

"Easy now," said Paul. "This isn't an uncommon delusion. Mary Tudor was convinced of her pregnancy for twice the normal term."

"Mary needed an heir," said Laura, "to block Elizabeth."

"True. But then, we don't know what Abigail's needs may have been. Let me read you the last passage in the journal:

"*September 5.* I remain firm in my Resolve to tell him nothing of my State. Therefore, I must very presently disappear from his sight lest his eyes—however fixed on his Armies and the Enemy—should inform him. I know not where I shall go. When I return he will have gone and have no occasion to see the child or question me. Beyond leaving him I regret most departing from this bed which held our Joy and now will hide this Record of it."

"But what happened?" asked Laura. "Did she have the child? Did he ever learn about it?"

Paul slowly raised his shoulders. "This journal may supply some clues to work on. Provided we find a record of Abigail. Or maybe, with this text in mind, new meaning will be given to hidden references in other records. It's a matter for historians now."

"Isn't it a matter for public knowledge, too?" asked Snaith.

"How can you tell the public about something that may never have happened?"

"By presenting it as . . . as just what it is—an interesting document of the time. Without claiming that it's true."

"Yes," said Paul, "you could do that."

"*Could* do that?" exclaimed Hester. "We *have* to do that. We can't mark the journal 'Top Secret.' What would we call it— the Morristown Papers?"

"As a matter of fact," said Paul, "I've already made this public, as a rumor."

"You did?"

"Yes. In court this morning. I found it necessary to give Annie Cobb the bare details."

"Why? Why Annie?"

"She was all excited about the fact that Laura is Jessica Conroy's daughter. She was going to focus her story on that, and she was hoping for the front page. I was afraid that angle would obscure the issue of freedom of expression."

"So you traded her?"

"Well, she said she'd try to play it way down if she couldn't suppress it, even though the story about Laura was bound to get to her husband—he publishes the paper—from someone else who'd been in court. But she agreed the journal story was bigger and she'd try to concentrate on that. You see, I rather agree with Hester that we have no right to make the journal a classified document, merely a responsibility to stress how unproven it is. The public has a right to know it exists."

"That's nothing but a news story," said Snaith contemptuously. "What I want to publish is the journal itself. With whatever disclaimers. As a matter of fact, sir, how would you like to write the introduction to it, with all the warnings of possible fiction you want?"

Paul cocked his head. "Let's shelve that for the moment until we see what Chayne comes up with. And what you find about a Lawrans family in your genealogies, Hester."

That was Wednesday. On Thursday, Judge Negley lifted the restraining order from *Ecstatic Excursions* and restored it to Hester's shelves. She also dismissed the charge against Tabard and Hester for distributing and circulating obscene material. Hester, meanwhile, searched diligently but found no reference to Abigail or any other Lawrans. And on Friday, *The Channel* made its weekly appearance. It hadn't carried an eight-column streamer since the disastrous floods of that June. But now, across its front page, it proclaimed:

LOCAL GIRL CLAIMS SHE'S
MOTHER OF HER COUNTRY

On its next-to-last page and well beneath the fold, a two-column head discreetly announced:

DAUGHTER VS PARENT
IN COURT PORN TILT

32

After lunch on Friday, *The Channel* was distributed to the homes of Mansfield. A few copies had appeared earlier on local newsstands. It wasn't until late afternoon that most readers, wondering what the banner headline meant, saw the story. Some read it with a mixture of amusement and disbelief, some with a curiosity its lack of detail scarcely satisfied, some dismissed it as a new-day Parson Weems fable. A few tossed it aside as a movie-magazine fan would turn from the warmed-over scandal of a silent-screen star. One rude fellow—a local reprobate—was heard to mutter after reading it, "There he goes, knocking over another cherry."

In her house on North Hill Road, Mrs. Laurens Lawrence read the headline with puzzled distaste, the story with anger and Abigail's surname with apprehension. Operating as usual on a firm but unthought-out impulse, she went to her writing table, picked up a pen and began: "To the Editor—" Then she put down her pen, went to her bookshelves and took down a well-thumbed Volume IV of *The History and Genealogy of the Families of Guernsey County New Jersey.* She searched for a "Lawrans" reference. But she found no more than had Hester. She then pulled out a lovingly worn history of Henry Laurens, President of the Continental Congress, and a slimmer tome, the memoirs of John Laurens, one of George Washington's most trusted aides and staff officers. She leafed through both of these, starting in each instance with the index. Whatever she was searching for was evidently not there and she seemed greatly relieved. She returned to her table and stared down at it, apparently considering the act of returning to her pen and notepaper. Then she turned from there and went out through the open French doors onto her broad pillared porch and sat for a long time, overlooking but not seeing her lawns, her maples, her laurels, her rose garden. What, she was wondering, should Mansfield's most prominent member of the Daughters of the American Revolution do?

Elsewhere in northwest Mansfield, Morley Oliver put down the paper whose lead story he had been reading for the second time. He chuckled, and going to the phone, called his favorite former employee, David Penn, who still was WLLD's late-evening-news commentator. "Dave, remember you were saying you'd like to get hold of an occasional lively item to put between the story of a tax debate and the latest garbage scandal? Well, if tonight's show isn't too tight already . . ."

At eleven-thirty a lady living in Lumberville, Pennsylvania, called the *New York Times* and asked for her son, who happened to be one of the assistants to the managing editor. "Sorry to bother you," she said, "but I was just listening to Dave Penn on WLLD. He says that the paper in Mansfield, New Jersey, has a weird story . . ."

At seven forty-five on Saturday morning, a one-time college roommate of Annie Cobb called her from New York. ". . . Yes, in the *Times* this morning. The Late City—on page fifteen . . ."

At eleven Mrs. Laurens Lawrence took the call from New York. "Oh, how did you hear about it? . . . In the *Times*! *They* would! . . . Well, of course I was upset. And I was going to write the Chapter about it . . . No. It didn't seem all that urgent . . . Really? A regional board meeting? . . . No, of course she was no relation—if she ever existed. No one in the family ever spelled it that way. And anyhow, Henry came from North Carolina. Yes, and John was born there, too. None of us came North until my grandfather, after the Civil War. Then his daughter—she was my aunt—married my husband's father. Of course they were both named Laurens—they were cousins. I know it was like *them*—but I can't help *that*!"

At eleven-twenty Annie Cobb called Paul De Witt. "Look!

I've just had a call from the *Times*—from New York. They wanted to know if I knew how the journal was discovered and where it was in your house. All you told me was in an antique and that's all I wrote. I should have asked you more about it. They'd called you, but you must have been out. What kind of furniture was it, Paul?"

"Oh, yes, Annie. Well, that detail seemed rather unimportant. And it can't matter to you now—your next issue won't be out for a week. You surely won't do a follow-up that long after."

"Oh, but we might. The *Times* wants to know. So *they're* doing a follow-up. It might not die so fast. Where was the thing anyhow?"

"In a bed."

"A bed!"

"Yes. A very old one. It broke."

"No!" exclaimed Annie, her voice charged with new excitement. "How? I mean who—I mean what *were* they doing?"

"Control yourself," said Paul, managing a dry, laconic tone. "It was nothing like what you seem to think." He cleared his throat while he wondered whether the American Historical Association had ever taken a position on white lies. "A guest entered the room in the dark. He tripped and fell on the bed, cracking some slats. That's where the journal had been hidden."

"Who was the guest?"

"Who? I'm not sure. I was putting up several people who'd been held over by the hearing."

"But whoever it was must have been upset. Surely you can remember who it was."

"We were all upset. And anyhow, I wasn't there when it happened. I was downstairs."

"Who was upstairs?"

"Quite a few, Annie. Let me think about it. If I remember, I'll call you back." He hung up quickly. After a moment he dialed Manhatten information and asked for the home telephone of Marc Holland. Somewhere on West Tenth Street, he thought.

When the reporter from the *Times* called Marc, he was given a smooth story neatly conformed to the version Paul had issued to Annie. The reporter was on the verge of hanging up when he asked, "Are you a personal friend of Paul De Witt?"

"Well, of course. I was staying in his house."

"Why were you down that way?"

"On legal business."

"Can you be a little more specific?"

"I could, but there'd be no point. It was something quite extraneous to the finding of the journal."

"Still . . ." Then: "Were you on a case? Something involving De Witt?"

"I'm afraid you'll have to excuse me. I'm already late for an appointment."

The *Times* reporter sat staring at his cradled phone. After a bit, he swiveled toward the girl at the adjoining desk. "Who lives around Mansfield, New Jersey—near Morristown—who'd be coming in this afternoon for the night shift?"

The girl looked at him and went on typing. He added, "I want someone to pick up a local paper."

"Why ask me? I'm not personnel."

"That's a thought," he said and lifted his phone again.

33

The driver helped Marc load the two suitcases into the front of his cab. Laura and he climbed into the back and the cab rolled away from the Barbizon toward Park and then south.

"You know," said Laura, "when I told Linc—"

"Oh. Now it's Linc. I remember when you barely managed Lincoln."

"I know. Being fellow houseguests changes things."

"Doesn't it, though. You were saying?"

"When I told him I was moving out of the Barbizon he didn't seem surprised."

"Did you think he would?"

"I thought he might ask for my new address. For the office records."

"He probably figured you'd fill that out yourself. And I'm sure he knows the address. He's been over more than once."

"Umm. For dinner?"

"Yes. Why?"

"I was wondering."

"Whether I can cook?"

"That, too. But whether Roz could."

"Stop being the new Mrs. De Winter."

"Who?"

"I know you're young. And I know it wasn't required reading for Lit majors. But didn't you ever watch the *Late Show?*" They were caught in the permanent traffic jam below Thirty-fourth. "Listen. Not that I'm looking for trouble, but suppose your mother called you at the Barbizon and found out you'd left?"

"I wrote her night before last. Incidentally, I'll have to add my name to your mailbox so the postman will know. I didn't happen to mention to Mother that it was in care of anybody."

"And if she comes to town and drops in sometime?"

She sighed. "Then she'll know."

"Would that be very bad? For you?"

"Oh. There'd be a tantrum." She seemed depressed, then brightening with an effort. "I'd tell her the simple truth."

"Such as?"

"Didn't I tell *you?* I'm accepting your suggestion that we live together. To see if I like it."

"And—just in case you do?"

"I might ask you to marry me. Or we might decide to leave well enough alone and just go on."

"In sin!" He pretended shock.

"Don't you think I've earned a little?"

The cab was inching through the crowds in Union Square. "After the virtue you've had to put up with? I think you've earned a lot." He jutted his jaw with manly determination. "And I'm going to see that you get it."

34

The Sunday *Times* carried the follow-up. Not a big story. Not yet.

Laura and Marc read it over a late and leisurely breakfast. It seemed that a journal had been found in an antique bed in the home of Professor Paul De Witt in Mansfield, New Jersey.

The journal had been secreted in the slats and fallen out when a clumsy ("You really aren't," said Laura) guest ("At least they kept it singular," said Marc) stumbled and fell on the bed. The journal appeared to have been kept by an Abigail Lawrans in 1777 who suggested that she had been the mistress of an American commanding officer who sounded very much like George Washington. There was a further strong suggestion that he was responsible for her pregnancy. Professor De Witt had said he was unable to testify to the genuineness of the journal and added that it was currently being examined by Dr. Henry Chayne of Princeton, who, when asked, said it was too early to be certain, but that the ink and paper—on preliminary tests —seemed old enough to be authentic. Professor De Witt was an important witness, the day after the journal was found, in a pornography case brought by local members of Americans for Clean Entertainment against the Mansfield library on charges that a volume, *Ecstatic Excursions,* displayed and circulated there and published by Tabard Press, contained obscene material. A witness for the defense had been Miss Laura Conroy, an employee of Tabard Press, who admitted that she wrote material for books of the same type as that named in the complaint. Miss Conroy was the daughter of Jessica Carroll Conroy, president of Americans for Clean Entertainment. Reached at her home in Ludgrove, Ohio, Mrs. Conroy had refused comment.

The phone was ringing. Laura looked startled and Marc, going to the phone, said, "I guess that's her comment now."

But the call wasn't from Jessica. Rupert and Jenny, in their Bucks County weekend place, had seen the *Times* and wanted a complete fill on the details. Marc started to comply when Laura suggested that if they were coming into town that evening, they stop off for drinks and a deli supper.

"They'll have an extra girl with them," said Marc. "I said to bring her along."

Less than an hour later Lincoln Snaith called from Connecticut, where he'd been staying overnight. He wondered what his story should be, how much detail he should supply if the *Times* called him on Monday. He assumed they'd been after him already, but he'd been away since late Friday. So he, too, was asked to drop in if he felt like dropping in. He felt like it.

Laura grabbed the phone. "And, Linc, there'll be an extra girl for you."

"Now, cut it out," said Snaith, "you're new to this game. Nobody's ever managed to match me up. I'm invulnerable."

Afterwards Laura asked, "What about Linc and women? Has he ever been married?"

"No. And don't ask me about his girl friends. If he's had them—and I assume he has—he's kept them and it to himself."

"Maybe," said Laura, "he's asexual. Or homosexual."

"I doubt the former. And I've never seen the slightest indication of the latter."

"Maybe he doesn't go for lawyers. How can you tell, anyhow?"

"Sometimes it's difficult—if it isn't overt."

"Isn't it usually? Overt I mean."

Marc shrugged. "The ones we can recognize are overt—mostly. The covert homosexual is naturally hard to detect—if anyone wants to bother. Doesn't the same go for lesbians?"

"Maybe. I'm not sure I ever met one. That's something else I've never tried. Or wanted to"—she frowned thoughtfully, struggling with her new sense of sexual inquiry—"I guess." She brightened. "Oh well, one thing at a time."

35

Snaith arrived first. He'd been surprised by the number of paragraphs the story had been given in the Sunday *Times,* and even more by the avid interest its two aspects had aroused in his Connecticut host and hostess and their other guests. They had been equally intrigued by "What kind of girl is Jessica Carroll Conroy's daughter?" and "Do you really believe Washington had that fling in New Jersey, and if he did, how could it have been concealed from the historians?" Snaith said he'd answered the first by saying Laura was a nice girl ("How dull," said Marc. Laura said, "That was last week"), and the second by saying experts were trying to clarify that very issue. But their interest in the journal had delighted him and made him even more determined to publish it—whether as historical document, Freudian fantasy or ancient prank.

Marc was just reassuring Lincoln that in his opinion, Paul had the right to convey its publication rights, when Rupert and Jenny arrived with Toni Faust. Ten years before, Toni had been publicity director of Rupert's firm. Tiring of what she'd often been heard to call "the Christ-awful business of trying to do a decent job on the media while simultaneously acting as travel and booking agent, routing authors from city to city, seeing to it that nobody screws up the plane and hotel reservations, scheduling them from local talk shows to bookstore autographing parties, to Book and Author luncheons, making certain that time is left for them to enplane for their next city, and all the while bugging the sales department to make sure that there are books to autograph at every appearance, and meanwhile trying to make it clear to various editorial colleagues that how the hell can a girl help it if yesterday's author interview appeared below the fold of the Woman's Page in the Washington *Post,* or last week's practically promised *Time* cover story was killed because some mad fool at *Time* considered it less important than the sudden weekend disappearance of half of Antarctica beneath a tidal ice wave," she'd finally quit the book business and retired to the relative peace and quiet and doubled salary of the TV talk-show world. Nowadays she was one of the four talent co-ordinators of Steve Molding's five-nights-a-week ninety-minute network talk show, which (not counting inexplicable pre-emptings) had miraculously survived provable contentions of frequent intellectual content, warnings that it was overshooting the flatter heads, and the damnable fact that Molding had attended a quite good college which had failed to diminish his love of literature, his original wit or his ease among the polysyllabic. As a talent co-ordinator, it was Toni's job to pre-interview potential guests and supply Molding with estimates of their conversational abilities and areas of knowledge. She was constantly on the lookout for new topics, and in the morning's *Times,* she'd found two. Now she deliberately faded into the background, listened and observed while the conversation developed several points of interest to her:

This girl, Laura, was quite pretty and probably telegenic. She seemed fairly unselfconscious and unlikely to freeze under the lights. And, Toni was reasonably certain, no talk show had ever interviewed an RSV girl.

As for the other topic, Toni had already made up her mind to suggest Paul De Witt for the show again. He had appeared twice before—once when the second volume of his Sam Adams was published (Molding and Paul had enjoyed developing a line connecting campus unrest to the Boston Tea Party), and later when Molding just wanted to share the pleasure of Paul's company with his audience. Now, Toni felt, Paul could come on as present owner of the journal, as an authority on the period of its presumed writing—and hadn't the *Times* mentioned that Paul had been an expert witness in that Jersey pornography trial? Maybe the stories—Laura and Paul on erotica, Laura on defying her mother's organization, Paul on the journal (maybe Laura had been around when it was found: the *Times* had said people connected with the porn trial were at his home at the time)—might all add up to quite a show, maybe the whole ninety minutes.

Around eight-thirty Marc answered the phone in his bedroom. He emerged wearing a peculiar expression.

"It's for you," he said to Laura, and when she passed him in the doorway and asked "Mother?" he nodded. He closed the bedroom door and returned to the living room. Toni was asking Snaith about his books, particularly his Solus books. He was answering with a warmth she'd often encountered in people trying to get on the show, and in men trying to get on with her. Snaith wasn't too easy to place in either category. Nor could he tell whether she was as interested in him as she seemed, or merely in a possible Molding guest.

In the bedroom Laura had picked up the phone. "Hello, Mother."

"That was your Mr. Holland, wasn't it?"

"Yes. It was."

"You carefully neglected to mention him when you sent me the phone and address. Just as you omitted telling me what kind of work you were doing at Tabard Press."

"I know. But in neither case was it cowardice. I saw no reason to upset you."

"Hmmm. Would you be surprised to know that I'm at least as upset by the nature of your work as I am by your living with a man?"

"Yes. I am surprised."

"You've never understood me, Laura. I knew when you left home, came to New York, this could happen. I hate it. But I'm not blind to what is going on in the world. Or to your weakness. I'm aware of what you young people call the new life style."

"I'm delighted to hear it."

"Don't be. I'm not approving it, God knows. I merely know I can't fight it. It's *your* life." Her mother paused. "But when you take a hand in affecting other people's lives, the whole society, by creating and spreading filth—that I cannot and will not accept."

"I'm sorry that's the way it seems to you. And if you have to fight what I'm doing in my job, I can't do anything but fight back. When you see the New York papers—"

"I've seen the *Times*."

"How did it get out there so fast?"

"It didn't. I'm in New York. At the Comstock. I want you to come up here. This evening."

Laura said nothing for some moments.

"Mother."

"Yes."

"Look. I spent almost my whole life till now absorbing your environment. I know it very well. And I respect it—for you. But now I've got an environment, and I want you to see it. And some friends I've made who are here now. I want you to meet them. Not across a courtroom, but in my home. It is my home, Mother. Mine and Marc's. Whatever you wanted to say to me at the Comstock you can say down here. I promise you a respectful audience. And, Mother, I want to be your hostess. You taught me how to be that. And I'm grateful to you. We're having deli food, but I can fix you an omelet or whatever else you'd prefer."

"Thank you, no. I've had dinner." There was a long pause. Laura wondered if they were still connected. Then her mother spoke, firmly: "Can I take a bus?"

"Yes." Laura felt a nervous joy. "But don't. Take a cab. It's after dark and this is New York."

"That's what I tried to tell you—two months ago."

When Laura returned to the living room, she said to Marc, "Mother's coming down. She'll be here soon."

Rupert started to say something. Snaith rose.

"I invited her," Laura continued, "to see where I live and to meet my friends. So please relax. It will help me to."

"Why is she in New York?" asked Marc. "I thought she was calling from Ludgrove."

"So did I. She isn't so furious about my being here—it's my job that she can't take. There's something she wants to say. And I intend to listen."

"But what? Why does she have to?" Marc was dismayed.

Rupert chuckled. "The First Amendment, old fellow."

"Yes," said Laura, "exactly."

"I wonder," Toni murmured, "if there's anything she'd like to say on the air."

36

What you do when you live on the second floor of a New York brownstone and want to extend old-world welcome-to-the-manor courtesies to an arriving guest is watch through the front window of your apartment until you see the approaching equipage and then race like hell down the stairs and out the front door. Thus, as Jessica Conroy finished paying her taxi driver and began to step out of the cab, Laura and Marc suddenly appeared on the sidewalk, Marc holding the cab door open while Laura extended her hand and cheek.

Jessica, who'd won and kept her cool long before the expression passed into the vernacular, managed to alight without either using or obviously spurning Laura's hand and permitted herself to be held momentarily in a light embrace while appearing merely to be glancing up and down the brownstone façade as though she suspected its hem of being crooked. She replied to Marc's "Welcome, Mrs. Conroy" with a nod which committed her to no more than having heard him, and imperceptibly wiggling her elbow from Laura's hand, descended the two steps toward the American basement entrance. She passed through the door Marc held for her, stepped across the vestibule with a glance at the mailboxes on her right, paused as Laura opened the snap-lock inner door, and walked along the hall with only a faintly raised eyebrow as indication that she'd noted the key with which Laura had done it and which, in her key container, she still held in her hand.

They stood, a silent threesome, while Marc pressed the button and a clank and wheeze from somewhere above suggested that an elevator was painfully descending. Laura inquired about her father. Jessica appeared absently to recall that he was well. The elevator door slid open and the two of them crowded into the tiny cage. Marc walked leisurely up the stairs and was waiting for them as they arrived on the floor above. He pushed open an apartment door forward of the elevator and Jessica stepped into a small foyer to find herself face to face with a delicately drawn, diaphanously veiled, erotically curvaceous Aubrey Beardsley nude. Jessica allowed two little lines between her brows to assert that she knew a dirty picture when she saw one. Marc, noting the lines, decided there was no point in explaining the picture as the high-camp it had been when he'd hung it there some years before.

Laura led her mother into the living room, where Jessica coolly accepted the introductions to Rupert, Jenny, Toni and Snaith with a pursed-lipped haughtiness which might have meant merely that she'd recognized the names of both men from courtroom clashes—or that she was relieved and surprised to find all present fully clothed.

Jessica Conroy, whatever one might think of her cause, was a pro. Possibly, even, a champ. From a platform, she could be scathing, or if the occasion demanded, violent. In private she could be bitter, accusing, threatening. But this was a social situation, and without acceptance or rejection, she met it. And it wasn't an easy one for her to meet. First had been the encounter downstairs with Marc: in the simplest terms—and Jessica seldom used other—the seducer of her virgin daughter. Now, here were Rupert Hayes and Lincoln Snaith, Jr.: the former a lapsed Ohioan who had become the publisher of Priam Wendell's obscure erotica, the latter the wretched sponsor of those unspeakable Solus books and the man who'd lured her daughter into literary prostitution. As for Jenny and Toni —all she knew about the former was that Rupert had met her in the dubious environs of some Boston graduate school, and married her a suspiciously long time thereafter; and this Miss Faust—well, Faust did sound faintly foreign, possibly Jewish, or at the very least, involved with Satan and the opera.

But none of this showed as she accepted a chair, heard Marc's suggestion of iced tea or ginger ale and Laura's offer to select some meats and salad from platters arranged on a long table against the wall. Jessica refused them both and looked past them toward the front wall lined from floor to ceiling, around and over its two curtained windows, with crowded bookshelves. She couldn't identify any of the volumes from where she sat, and possibly, was willing to accept them as innocent until proven guilty.

"I hope you'll be able to stay in New York for a while," Laura was saying.

Jessica shook her head. "Only until tomorrow. I'm on my way to Washington. This morning, after I'd heard the radio news, I decided to come here first."

Jenny observed that Washington could be frightfully hot this time of year and Jessica, agreeing, said the hearing room was air-conditioned. She returned her gaze to the shelves, counting on Laura to ask the obvious question.

"What hearing room, Mother?"

"Congressman Tobler's. His subcommittee of the Post

Office Committee," said Jessica. She didn't wait for another cue. "The one that's taking a new look at postal rates. They've decided to examine the rates for educational materials—" She glanced expectantly at Laura, who remained silent. So Jessica added, "—which include books." She looked brightly at the three men.

Rupert said rather wearily, "I hadn't heard that they were looking at *those* rates again."

"They weren't, Mr. Hayes. They are now. They're wondering if books deserve the special mailing privileges they've been enjoying."

Snaith glanced at Rupert. Rupert looked at Marc. Marc looked resigned. Then he smiled. "Why tip us off? Now publishers can try to rally a defense."

Jessica smiled back coldly. "Of course. We want the issue out in the open. It's time taxpayers knew of the special considerations being extended to you people. After all, taxes still have to make up post-office deficits, even now that the department is theoretically run as a separate business."

"I suppose, Mother, when you say 'we want' you mean—"

"I mean lots of people who are sick and tired of supporting the dissemination of pornography. Americans for Clean Entertainment is only one such group. Many of us are appearing as witnesses." She looked squarely at Marc. "Actually, this is why I accepted Laura's invitation tonight. I wanted you to know this. I hoped you'd tell your publishing clients. I didn't know that some of them would be here. The more you oppose the aims of this inquiry, the more attention it will get. And incidentally, the easier our fund-raising will be."

"Would you like to get it a lot of attention—right away?"

Jessica turned to Toni, who was leaning forward eagerly. "How do you mean? Are you in publishing too?"

"Not now. I'm in TV. If you were invited, would you be willing to appear on a network talk show?"

Jessica studied her. "Which one?"

"Steve Molding's."

Jessica grimaced. "I thought you'd say that. No. That's not the audience we're looking for. He doesn't really reach the people, you know."

"Why not? He even comes from your state."

"I know. And I don't think he's ever returned. No, we're not particularly interested in the so-called young intellectuals. We don't expect agreement from big cities and campuses. We want a more middle, more stable audience. Kit Kearney's or Leo Hawk's shows reach more of the *real* people—the one's we're representing."

"Representing?" Laura exclaimed. "Or trying to lead?"

"Actually," said Jessica, "both. We're representing those who understand the problem, and we're trying to lead the one's who aren't yet aware of it."

"Mother, the last time we were together, you suggested that if I stayed in New York, and at Tabard Press, and kept up other associations, you might—I forget exactly how you put it—make me wish I hadn't. Are you really going to all this trouble just to try to get me out of here?" She made a gesture which might have indicated the whole city or merely the flat.

"My dear Laura. I'm afraid you are flattering yourself. And demeaning the work I am doing. You've never understood its importance. Or its necessity. It began long before you ever thought of leaving Ludgrove. It will continue much longer than any activity you happen to be engaged in, now that you —I haven't forgotten *your* words—are twenty-two."

Laura sat silently for some moments, then she got to her feet. "Look, Mother, I didn't invite you down to quarrel with you. Truly. But I do want you to know something, though. The fact that I hope to go on working for Mr. Snaith, as long as he wants me to"—she paused and smiled—"adding very proper passages to those you'd consider improper, and the fact also that I intend to continue sharing this flat as long as it seems agreeable to the only parties concerned—neither of those facts is meant to defy you. I'm doing what I do because I want to. Not because you don't want me to."

"Oh, I quite understand that, Laura. And I agree, you're twenty-two and that gives you certain legal privileges. Actually, by today's permissive legislation, you've had them since you were eighteen. Well"—she sighed—"I make no secret of the fact that I'm forty-eight. It's possible that in my additional twenty-six years I've picked up some wisdom you don't enjoy."

Nobody said anything. Laura turned to the table and absently put a potato chip into some dip, muttering something about wisdom not being the only enjoyment.

Jessica rose and went over to the books. For long moments she seemed to be studying them, her eyes going from shelf to shelf. "Ah"—she was touching a forefinger to each of several adjacent volumes—"Paul De Witt. I heard about . . . about that so-called diary that was found in his house. What do you know about it? I'm interested." She turned and faced them.

Snaith started to speak, but Marc forestalled him. "Not very much, Mrs. Conroy. Several of us were there at the time. But I'm the only one who saw it. Very briefly."

"Of course it's a libel." She looked around again. "I hope you agree to that, at least."

Marc tilted his head with a ghost of a shrug. "It may be. Experts are examining it now."

"But it does sound interesting," said Snaith.

Jessica seemed to be studying him and his comment. "There must be defenses against such libels. Even for a dead man. And certainly for a dead hero." Her eyes contracted as if with serious thought. Watching Marc, she continued, "I must inquire about that in the next day or two. Joshua Tobler would know." She looked briefly at her wrist and then, doubtfully, around the group. "I have an early flight tomorrow. Perhaps someone could get me a cab."

"Mother. Marc and I will take you up—"

"No. Thank you. I insist. You must stay with your friends."

37

Marc and Laura came back into the apartment from their taxi-hailing chore. Rupert stopped reading aloud from a book in his hands and said to Marc, "I've borrowed your *Congressional Directory*. Congressman Tobler seems to be a neighbor of yours, Laura."

"A neighbor! If he doesn't come to Sunday dinner once a month, Mother thinks she's lost control of the government. I'm supposed to call him Uncle Joshua!"

Snaith asked, "Is he a member of A.C.E.?"

Laura nodded dubiously. "I think so. He's spoken at their conventions."

"I'm not sure that they can do much more than they've already done," said Marc; "the second-class rates are already out of sight and escalating. If they try to raise the book rate again, they'll have everyone from the National Education Association to the Association of American Publishers to the book clubs on their necks. My guess is that this is an A.C.E. fund-raising ploy and not much else."

"And not a ploy to get me out of here?"

"Honey, if you go out of here, you're not going to go as 'educational material.'"

"Educated material?" suggested Jenny.

"That's different," said Marc.

Snaith went to the long table and started to put a sandwich together. "Anyone see any evening news? I was wondering if the networks picked up that *Times* story."

Toni said, "I'd like to know that, too." She headed for the

bedroom. "Phone seems to be in here." Within a couple of minutes she emerged. "All three had it. NBC and ABC just covered the George and Abigail angle. CBS added a bit about you and your mother, Laura. So did CBS radio. I guess that's what your mother heard." She remained standing in the doorway as though undecided whether to return to the bedroom. "All three report inquiries coming in about the Lawrans journal. Mostly from magazine and newspaper people." She chewed at her lower lip. "That story may grow fast. And if it does, Steve Molding will want to cover it on his earliest possible show. Maybe even tomorrow." She looked at Snaith, then at Marc. "You did say that Paul De Witt owns the thing now?"

"As far as I know, yes," said Marc.

"I'd like to talk to him. Mind if I call from here?"

"Go right ahead," said Marc. "I don't know his number."

She took a large loose-leaf notebook from her purse. "If you were ever on the Molding show, you're in here—and Paul was." She turned into the bedroom again, but before she could pick up the phone, it rang. Automatically she reached for it, then drew back her hand. She was still standing by it when Marc came past her and lifted the receiver. "Hello . . . No. She just left . . . Yes, possibly. Who is this? . . . Oh, well—how did you get this number? . . . I see. Would you hold on a minute?" He went back into the living room and Toni followed him to the door. "Laura, there's someone from Conservative Controversy on the phone. They want to know where to reach your mother. Seems they called Ludgrove and your father gave them the Comstock's number and the Comstock had this one. Shall I tell them she's gone back there?"

"Sure. If Daddy gave them that number in the first place . . ."

Marc went back to the phone.

"That wasn't 'someone' from Conservative Controversy," said Toni. "I was standing right next to the phone. I'd know that tenor voice anywhere. That was Sam Shield himself."

Marc, returning to the living room, said, "I know it was.

And he may have recognized my voice. I've tangled with him a couple of times." He rubbed his jaw. "So he wants your mother on his show—maybe he'll want you, too."

Before Laura could answer, Toni said, "Not a chance. He doesn't go after both sides of a question. If his guest is conservative, he joins in on his side. If he's radical, he takes on the argument himself."

"How big an audience has he?"

"Hard to measure," said Toni. "It's syndicated—not network." To Laura she said, "If Paul De Witt came on our show, would you come too? Especially if your mother did."

"Aren't the journal and the trial a couple of different subjects?"

"Maybe. But they're joined—by time, place, some of the cast of characters. Would you?"

"I don't know. I'd rather not. I don't want to argue with Mother. Certainly not publicly."

"But the media are making it public."

"They can't make a quarrel public. Because I'm not having one."

Toni was on the point of saying more, but she turned back into the bedroom. She remained there for something more than five minutes. When she emerged she held a notebook page in her hand, and referring to jottings on it, talked rapidly. "I spoke to Paul. So's everybody else this evening. *Time* called him. They're squeezing a double story into the issue they're closing tonight. About the journal. And about the library trial. They've interviewed Hester. They've been trying to reach you . . ." She looked up at Snaith. "They've picked up the angle about you and your mother, Laura. Paul says they sounded as though they wanted to kid the attack on those oldies—*Jurgen* and whatever the other books were. They wanted to reach you, Laura, about your job of writing in breathers. Paul told them he didn't know where you could be reached before tomorrow. Then he added to me that he knew you'd been at the Barbizon but wasn't so sure you still were."

Marc said, "He's got beautiful instincts."

"Paul says that right after *Time* called, he heard from *Newsweek*," Toni continued. "It seems they're mostly interested in the journal. They want to do a feature story with reproductions of pages from the thing. And pictures of Paul's house and the antique bed, and when Paul kept insisting that nothing was really proven about the journal yet and he didn't want the public jumping to unfounded conclusions, they asked him to do a signed piece as an insert for their story telling exactly what's known, what's conjecture and how contrary Abigail's account is to what's on record about Washington."

"Is he going to do it?" asked Snaith.

"Probably. He says if they're going to run a story, he wants to cool it way down."

Snaith jumped up and paced the room. "Damn. I've got to talk to Paul. I *have* to publish that journal and I want him to do the foreword—he can base it on what he's going to do for *Newsweek*." He started toward the bedroom. "I'm going to call him and try to see him tomorrow."

"Relax," said Toni. "You are seeing him tomorrow. Let me finish. Right after *Newsweek* got through talking to Paul, Molding called him. Steve's scrapping tomorrow night's scheduled show, or postponing it anyhow. And he's going to do a whole ninety minutes devoted to the trial and the journal. He wants Paul, he wants that librarian, Hester something—Paul's calling her right now. He wants you, Lincoln. He wants that author of yours, the one who wrote *Lay On, Miss Baxter* or whatever it's called. And he wants you, Laura, to talk about writing in those what-to-do-before-anyone's-coming scenes. Now I've got to call him because he's probably been trying to reach me all evening. And when I do, he's going to ask me to get hold of your mother. I'm sure of it. Unless he's had someone else on the wire to Ludgrove and traced her to the Comstock."

"She won't go on his show," said Laura. "You heard her say so. She hates his show. She calls him a liberal egghead."

"I didn't know she'd use such dirty language. Anyhow, I'm calling Steve now. Okay?"

After Toni returned to the bedroom there was a moment's quiet, which Rupert broke. "She didn't ask if you'd go on, Linc —or you, Laura. She just assumed it."

"I think she has a right to," said Snaith. "She heard me say I want to publish the journal. She's got to figure I'll help get it publicity."

"But what about Laura?" asked Jenny. "I mean, would you go on, Laura?"

"That depends," Laura said. "I'll go on and say what I said in court. But I won't go on and get into a fight with Mother. Or even about Mother."

"But suppose she's there . . . on the show?" asked Jenny.

"She won't be. Sam Shield's, yes. Steve Molding's—not a chance."

And when Toni returned she quickly confirmed Laura's judgment. "Your mother said absolutely not. Then I asked her if she was going on any other interview show and she became suspiciously noncommittal. Just before she hung up, she asked if you were going on the Molding show."

"What did you tell her?"

"I said I didn't know. Then I asked if she'd mind your appearing and she hemmed and hesitated and then said I'd have to forgive her but she was working on her testimony for the hearing tomorrow."

"That," said Laura, "was her answer."

"Oh. Translate it for me."

"She was saying that the more publicity I give the trial—or the journal, I suppose—the tougher she'll come down on por-nography and the book postal rates."

"Like that, huh? So now maybe I'd better ask you—will you join the little party tomorrow?"

Laura looked at Rupert and Snaith. "I will, unless a couple of publishers think they'd rather I didn't make Mother tougher to get along with."

"I'm afraid your mother will always be tough to get along with, even if she isn't given additional cause," said Rupert. "I hate blackmail."

"Hell," said Snaith, "I'll order you to appear—Solus Books need publicity."

"But remember," Laura said to Toni, "I'm not going to talk about anything except my job, and how I feel about censorship. Any discussion of Mother is off-limits. Understood?"

Toni crumpled the notepaper she'd been holding and tossed it into a wastebasket. "You can tell that to Steve before the taping. He'll understand. You'll be surprised what a decent guy he is. *But*—he's certainly got to say whose daughter you are. For God's sake, that's been all over the news."

"He can say whatever he wants. I'm just not going to talk about Mother's crusade, or whatever you want to call it, or anything about Mother and me." She lapsed into momentary silence. Then she suddenly grinned. "I'll just take the Fifth. And not the Amendment. The Commandment."

38

Shortly before midnight on Monday, some fifteen million Americans had their first look at Abigail Lawrans' journal.

Paul had been reluctant to bring it to the studio for the taping at six o'clock that day. But he'd arrived with it in a neatly ribbon-tied package and the explanation that Princeton —or at least Harry Chayne—had finished with the physical tests and photocopied the entire contents. "And, anyhow, I've never lost a book yet, none that I didn't want to."

Now, on screen, Steve Molding was reaching for it as Paul undid the ribbon and wrapping and passed the slim volume across to him. Steve, holding the book gently, carefully opened it. A TV camera on his left was moving in. "I don't know whether this will be clear on your home screens, but at least you'll get some idea of the handwriting."

On the little color set drawn up at the foot of Marc's bed the image shifted to a close-up of the journal.

"I can't make out a word," said Laura.

"No," answered Marc, "we couldn't read anything up in the control room this afternoon."

Molding was looking up at Paul. "It's eerie to realize that these words were written one hundred and ninety-five years ago . . ."

". . . and now are being seen on sets three thousand miles away."

"Miss Lawrans has conquered time and space," said Molding. "Or was she Mrs. Lawrans?"

"The journal doesn't say. She *might* have been wife or widow."

"But not, according to her testimony, maid." Steve hesitated. "Maybe I ought to spell that. What would you guess this is worth, Paul?"

Paul pursed his lips. "Anyone who put a price on it at this point would be gambling. It may be just a curiosity—a two-century-old hoax. It may be a scandalous bit of history."

"But there's no question about its age—about it really being written during the American Revolution?"

"About its age—no question. But the paper and ink tests—and they've all stood up—aren't that precise. It might have been written a decade or so later."

"But not earlier."

"Not unless Abigail was a clairvoyant. If the British couldn't foresee the crossing at Trenton, I don't think she could have."

"Do the tests show anything else about this?" He weighed the book in his hands.

"About the physical property? No. But about the writer—about Abigail—yes, a little. For instance, there's no doubt that it was written by a woman, and probably a young one."

"How can you tell that?"

"I can't. It's not my field. But several experts are reasonably sure about the handwriting . . . its characteristics. It's firm, yet delicate, and there's no sign of tremor in the end strokes. Hence, they tell us, someone not old, someone female."

"Anything about her position in society? Her education?"

"Her usages and spelling are good. They stand up with the upper-middle society of her time. She certainly had some schooling—or anyhow, tutoring. She probably was reasonably well read."

"Anything about her, or her family?"

"Nothing. Not yet. If we accept her words in there, she lived in New Jersey near Morristown in the spring and summer of 1777. She may have been there in the preceding indefinite period. A year before, she was in—lived or visited in—Camden. Or perhaps across the river in Philadelphia. At least there's a reference to a romantic, anyhow a sexual, episode in Camden in early July of 1776."

"Maybe," said Steve, "she was celebrating the signing."

"She suggests it was on the *eve* of the Fourth—a slightly earlier human event."

"And George III wasn't taxing *that*?" said Steve.

"Even a Lord North couldn't have been that frigid."

"Or else there might have been a Boston Sex Party." He looked into the camera with an innocent expression. "We'll be back after a word from—what a coincidence—a tea sponsor."

As the picture went to black, Laura pushed Marc's hand away. "Stop that. I want to see the whole show."

"Weren't you watching backstage?"

"Yes. But I want to see me."

"You don't come on yet."

"Stop it. I want to see it all. Dispassionately."

After the commercial break Steve, still holding the journal, said, "What's your guess, Paul—could this girl's claims be true?"

Paul shifted into a less relaxed position. "First of all, Steve, her claims aren't spelled out. She implies that she had an affair with someone in a distinguished position. Someone with 'Headquarters' in Morristown. Someone whose 'wife and ladies' visited him in April–May of that year. Someone with grave responsibilities to 'his Army' and great concern about 'the enemy.' "

"Do you know of anyone other than Washington who fills all those particulars?"

"No. No one that high whose wife and entourage were there then. But that brings us to a much stickier point. Was Abigail telling the truth? Or merely imagining?"

"And have we any hope of finding out more about her?"

"Maybe. It's impossible to say. A search is on—I imagine that there isn't a scrap of documentation of that period and that part of the country that won't be re-examined."

"How long might that take?"

"Anything from a few weeks to a century. After you've gone past the usual sources, town records, church records, genealogies, and re-examined *The Heads of Families of Guernsey County, First Census 1790*—"

"But that was after the date of this—"

"True. But it was the first official census. The British never made a reliable one. There's always the possibility of finding a clue in that to some members of her family—something that wouldn't be in a genealogy." Paul took a breath. "And then, after you've studied *The History of Mansfield*, which was published on its bicentennial back in 1935, you begin going through the correspondence and diaries of everyone who might have employed, been employed by, gossiped about or heard of a young lady of New Jersey in the 1770's."

"And if you find nothing?"

"Then you have negative proof."

"So that, without any record coming to light, she might have existed and her story could have been true?"

"That's right."

"But what about all the records of Washington's life?"

"There I can answer with more certainty, and not out of my own relatively meager knowledge. No respected biographer of Washington, not Freeman, or Flexner, or Nevins—not one of them suggests that Washington ever strayed from his marital vows to Martha."

Steve started to say something, but Paul went on, "Now, remember, George Washington was no stuffed shirt. He liked women, he was gallant to women, he enjoyed their society. As a young man he was known to have had close and passionate attachments. At least one of them seems to have been intense, long-lived and mutual. But that was before he married Martha Custis."

"So—aren't you saying Abigail's claim is untrue?"

"No. I'm saying that no proof of infidelity is known to me, and more important, to the eminent scholars who have specialized in his life. But no historian can declare that one, perhaps a very discreet one, can't or won't turn up." He pointed to the journal in Steve's hands. "Or hasn't."

Steve looked down at the volume. "Will this go into a museum? I suppose it could hardly make the National Archives."

"I don't know where it will end up. I'm told it's legally mine. All I can say now is that I want it to be available to the public under whatever label it turns out to deserve. Right now it's about to go on temporary display in the Mansfield Public Library."

It was after the next commercial break, after the introduction of Hester and Snaith, Jorgenson and Laura, that television history nearly was made. Steve Molding had led Hester through a quick review of the trial of *Ecstatic Excursions* and involved her with Paul in a brief résumé of famous book bannings, in the midst of which Hester suddenly burst out, "Why, it's hard to believe that only a few years ago they banned *Lady*

Chatterley's Lover just because it referred to the heroine's *bleep* as a *bleep*.*"*

The camera, withdrawing as if in shock, revealed Steve's face. He managed to keep it reasonably unstartled and straight. The studio audience gasped and then—at least the younger two thirds of it—exploded with laughter.

"What were the rest of you onstage doing?" asked Marc. "I was watching Molding."

"I don't know about the others. I blushed. I didn't dare look anywhere except at my lap."

"The subject having come up."

"Oh, shut up. Hearing that in a living room is one thing, but with those cameras and microphones . . ."

Marc chuckled.

"Don't laugh at me."

"I'm not. I was thinking of Max Levin."

"Why Max?"

"Those bleeps. Do you realize that television has invented a euphemism for which Max couldn't possibly give the linguistic basis?"

"That's true," said Laura. "Last week—the day he was working at Tabard—he told us all about William Dunbar."

"Who's he?"

"A fifteenth-century Scottish poet. It seems he's immortalized in the *New Supplement to the Oxford English Dictionary* as the first man in literature to use 'fuck' in a line of poetry. Only, he spelled it f-u-c-k-e."

"Just wanted it to last longer, I guess."

Steve had quickly switched his attention to Lincoln Snaith and Jorgenson and to the somewhat safer subject of the place of erotica in literature.

"But what," he finally asked, "about really hard-core pornography—stuff written badly and only to arouse?"

"I don't write it," said Jorgenson.

"I don't publish it," said Snaith.

"But aren't such books sold in the same shops that sell

yours? Including sleazy ones on Forty-second Street here in New York, for instance? Next to stag-film movie houses, in a district notorious for prostitutes, pimps, drugs?"

"That's true," said Jorgenson, "some of my books are sold there. And if the police want to clean up prostitution and those kind of stores and movie houses, let them—if they don't infringe on my constitutional rights."

"But can they, without infringing?"

"I don't know," said Snaith. "I'm not a lawyer. All I demand is the right to publish my books."

Paul spoke up and the camera shifted to him. "In line with the last point, I have a clipping here." He reached into his pocket. "I'd like to read three short excerpts from a letter that appeared in the *New York Times*. May I, Steve?"

"Of course. Please."

("I meant to ask him how he got hold of that clipping," said Laura. Marc said, "You should have asked me. I gave it to him just before you all went on. I thought it might be worked in —and the man who wrote it was one of my favorite teachers.")

"This letter," Paul was saying, "was written to the *Times* by a professor of law at Harvard. He was commenting on the current drive to clean up Times Square. At one point he writes about the objectionable posters on the street in front of pornographic bookshops and blue-film houses and he says: 'The externals of a movie house or bookstore can properly be regulated . . .' In the next paragraph he writes: 'But what goes on inside the movie theater or bookstore among consenting adults is, simply put, none of anybody's business.' At the end of his letter he says: 'The lesson of history has been that in the long run, a regime of censorship is far more dangerous to the values we all share.' And when he said 'far more dangerous' he was referring to the present clamping down on theaters and bookstores on Forty-second Street."

Paul put away the clipping and straightened in his leather chair. "I'm no more a lawyer than Mr. Snaith, but I've some knowledge of social history. And I know of no banning of truly disgraceful stuff—and there's no denying it has always existed—that hasn't eventually infringed on acceptable and often valuable entertainment. Not only the kind of robust books that Mr. Jorgenson writes, but even far milder examples." Paul hesitated for a moment. "That's why I oppose *all* censorship."

"Anyhow," said Jorgenson, "my books have lots of redeeming social value."

Steve turned to him. "Yes. That brings us to another point. You don't write those parts yourself, do you?" He looked across to Laura and she was given her first close-up.

("You look great." "That's make-up." "I don't mean the color. I mean the cheekbones." "That's partly make-up, too— shadow." "Nuts. I can *feel* your cheekbones." "That's a change, anyhow.")

"You write those redeeming sections, don't you, Miss Conroy?"

"Yes. I do now."

"To make the books publishable."

"Not just that. To make them better balanced, too. Not one-track."

"Some people say they're there just to get them past the law."

"I know some people say that."

Molding looked into a camera. "Before we went on this evening, Miss Conroy urged me not to raise the subject of her mother, who is widely known to oppose her work, and the field in which she is employed. Others have already recently raised the subject. But I find her reluctance to discuss it reasonable and honorable. So we won't. But"—he turned again to Laura—"some people take exception to your work. How do you feel about it?"

Laura looked at him candidly. "At first it was just a job. And I needed one. But then—I liked the people I was working with, and their friends. And I found I often enjoyed reading the kind of books I was working on."

"You mean erotic books?"

"Yes."

"Hadn't you ever read them before?"

"No, I'd never seen—I wasn't per—I didn't know they existed."

"But, Miss Conroy . . ." Molding hesitated, puzzled. "Without getting into personalities, you knew of at least one organization opposed to erotic books. What kind did you think they were?"

"I really didn't know. I guess I just didn't think about it. Or about a lot of things. To me, they were just books that people —some people—called 'dirty.' I didn't know of any difference between erotic and soft-core—or hard-core. I just thought some books were horrible things people were better off without."

"But you don't think that now?"

"No. Not since I've read some. Some *are* terrible—terribly written—dull, monotonous. Some are well written. And entertaining." Her jaw jutted and earnest lines creased her forehead. "But the—that organization you were talking about, it doesn't admit that there are any differences among them, not of worth or quality, or even degrees of what they call offensiveness." Her anger increased. "And now I know that some people connected with it call *Canterbury Tales*—the original uncut version—and parts of *Hamlet* and, I suppose, poems by Ovid and plays by Wycherly and Congreve—they call them all dirty." She was opening and closing her hands nervously. "And when some fat old creep I never hope to see again says things like that in a courtroom—well, that's one thing." She bit at her lower lip and then burst out, "But when—when someone you're supposed to respect—and love—says it . . ." She put the back of her clenched fist to her mouth and the camera picked up the sudden wetness of her eyes.

Molding quickly broke for a commercial.

When the program resumed, he said to a recovered Laura, "The passages you add to those books help make them legal, don't they?"

"Not where the obscenity laws don't have redeeming-social-value clauses. Like New Jersey. Yet a judge over there found it legal."

Paul stirred. "It's worth remembering that we had a reasonable and contemporary-minded judge. Another judge, under the illiberal Jersey statute, could have banned the book. Then the library would have had to appeal the case and there's no telling what would have happened."

Steve turned to Hester. "What effect will that judge's decision have on you? Will you put in more books like Mr. Jorgenson's?"

"Only if they stimulate reading, including other reading. And only if we have funds to spare. Right now, I'm thinking more about putting in extra copies of Washington biographies."

"Professor De Witt says you'll exhibit the journal."

"I think we should. Even if it's later exhibited in other places. We should show it first. It's home-grown."

"Suppose it isn't true?"

"We won't say it is. We can show it as possible apocrypha." She reflected. "Apocrypha has been made public before. Along with a lot of other unproven material."

Steve looked at her curiously. And decided not to pursue *that* line.

"I hope every word of it is true!" Jorgenson suddenly exclaimed.

Molding turned to him in some astonishment. "Why?"

"Because maybe it will shake us out of our smugness. The establishment needs shaking up. Like finding out that its pious beliefs about Washington—yes, and Lincoln too, and all the others—are a lot of myths."

"Myths!" exclaimed Molding "Washington fought and won the Revolution, he presided over the Constitutional Convention. Were those myths? Was Lincoln's determination to preserve the union a myth?"

"Maybe the need to was," said Jorgenson. "And as for the Constitution—maybe what it mainly does is protect property rights."

"It protects you. Your right to be published." Molding was cool. "Isn't that valuable to you?"

"Yes. But I'm not saying what I mean. I mean, maybe Lincoln shouldn't have preserved the Union. Maybe we'd be better off if the South had seceded."

"And you'd have been saying this over a lot fewer stations in a lot fewer states."

"Well, I don't mean just *those* things about the Establishment. I really mean the stuff that grew out of the myth—that Washington never told a lie or had a dame. Or that Lincoln always worked and studied when he was a kid and never was on the wrong side of an argument. Lots of that is myth. And it's being fed to everybody. And not just in school." Jorgenson took a deep breath. "Maybe this journal *should* be true so we'd know Washington was a human being. Not just a head up on Mount Rushmore."

"Cary Grant and Eva Marie Saint had to have *something* to climb down," said Steve. "Actually, wasn't there a book some years ago that tried to rub a lot of that virtue off of Washington?"

"There was," said Paul. "It was the first of what came to be called the 'debunking' books. But the one about Washington didn't do what Mr. Jorgenson seems to be hoping for. It made accusations that couldn't be proved."

"And the journal? Do you join Mr. Jorgenson in hoping that it will be proved true?"

"No. I just hope it turns out to be either provable or disprovable. And firmly so. One way or the other."

"And meanwhile?"

Paul shrugged. "A nine days' wonder, I should imagine. Then the excitement—whatever little there may be—will die down. And historians will enjoy peace and quiet to work on it. Maybe for years."

Molding considered this with a quizzically raised brow. "Meanwhile," he said, "we may get some mail. But first, a message from our sponsor."

39

On Tuesday, Lincoln Snaith received some phone calls. On
Wednesday the mail began to pile in to the network. (Toni
Faust phoned Snaith to tell him. "And," said Laura to Marc,
"he took her to lunch to talk about it." "That," answered
Marc, "is making the most of the mail prerogative.") On
Thursday the editorial comment began.

On Friday, Snaith phoned Paul.

"Paul, I want to get the journal out immediately. Will you
release it to me?"

"I told you I would. But what do you mean by 'immediately'?"

"I've been talking to the manufacturer I use for Solus Books.
They think they can get an edition out in a few weeks."

"That means paperback?"

"Yes. Just the text, plus your introduction. You will write
that, won't you?"

"I practically have. I can base it on this thing I'm doing for
Newsweek. But shouldn't this be a more permanent sort of
book? Hardcover? And with illustrations? Reproductions of
actual pages. Woodcuts or whatever of the Morristown-Mans-
field area . . ."

"That can be in a later edition. Right now I want to get out
the text while the interest is high. We can go into hardcover
later for the school and library market—with illustrations,
historical references, other apparatus. Paul, you've no idea
what's been going on here. Three major paperback houses
called me yesterday—after the Molding show."

"I know," said Paul. "They called me and I told them if anyone was going to publish it, I'd promised it to you."

"Believe me, I'm grateful," said Snaith. "Anyhow, they wanted to buy the rights from me. Their paperback edition instead of mine. They made some pretty good offers. Good enough to make me sure I wanted to do it myself, even if I netted more the other way. This could really establish the Solus line."

"And convince the bluenoses you'd gone from erotica to salacious scandal."

"I know. The Molding Show mail is splitting even between people who think it was a great program and people who think we were tearing down the country, beginning with the founding fathers. What got most of them mad was Jorgenson at the end. Paul, if we get this out soon enough it will cash in on something that's building fast."

"I'm sure that's fine from your standpoint. But I was thinking of a respectable hardbound book."

"Paul! Are you falling for the old line? What's respectable at seven ninety-five is objectionable at a dollar and a quarter?"

"N-o-o. But I'd rather see you issue it for scholars right now than for—" He paused. "I know, I know. It does sound like an elitist argument. And I'm not pleased with it. Nevertheless—"

"And you're doing a piece for *Newsweek*. That's no limited, scholarly market."

"Of course not. I only agreed to do that because they're covering the story anyway and I wanted to cool it down with some historical perspective and genuine doubts. But if I let you have the text and my introduction . . . No, I'm wrong. I'm practicing a form of censorship. I'm accepting the content and objecting to the container."

"Good. Now, suppose I told you I could pay a guarantee of twenty thousand dollars. That's not much in terms of big paperbacks, but I'm assuming this one is good for a couple-of-hundred-thousand sale."

"But it's public domain."

"Except that you own it. I deliberately didn't name a sum until you agreed to let me have it. I wouldn't like you to think I'm trying to bribe you."

"And I still wish you'd do the hardcover first. Give it a bookstore and library debut. Get it reviewed."

"We can't wait. Have you heard those editorials on the evening news shows?"

"Yes. But what do you think they were saying—besides 'on the other hand'?"

"That doesn't matter. It's important publicity. And that Washington columnist in the *Post?*"

"Ummm. He suggested that if he'd been alive in 1777, he'd have had the whole inside story from one of his Morristown sources."

"What's the difference? He's syndicated—big. And so's what's his name, that Broadway columnist. He's already wondering whether Abigail and other girls of that era really had D-cups or wore their corsets so high they just got pushed up that way."

"I can imagine," said Paul. His tone became serious. "Lincoln."

"What?"

"I've just reached one decision. I'll let you have the journal. But you can't pay me for it. I didn't create it. I didn't even find it. It was handed to me. By accident, as it were."

"Paul. That's very generous—"

"No, it's not. You're going to pay. But not me."

"Who then?"

Paul didn't answer him directly. Instead he said, "I'm thinking about that. I have to come to New York Monday. Will you be in your office—around two-thirty or three?"

"Sure. Could you bring me a photocopy of the journal then, too?"

"I'll have one for you. But remember, I still think it's a nine days' wonder—or maybe at most a nineteen-day one."

"I don't agree, Paul. Did you hear Jessica Conroy last night on the Sam Shield show?"

"Not listening to Sam Shield is one of my favorite diversions."

"Mine too, usually. But when I saw her listed in the TV program . . ."

"What did she say?"

"Well, first she was the stiff-upper-lipped, broken-hearted mother. She made no bones about discussing Laura and denouncing the influences which had—to use her word—'destroyed' her."

"And which influences were those? Did she say?"

"You bet she did. They're 'intellectuals' and 'certain kinds of New Yorkers' and 'the failure of our society to uphold standards of decency.' But all the way through, it was a skillful and bitter attack on Laura."

"How did she take it? I presume you've seen her."

"Sure. She's furious. Not so much at the implications about herself but at the attacks on the unnamed influences who Laura knows damn well are meant to be you and Marc —and me too, I suppose. Right now Laura's in an 'I never want to see or speak to her again' mood. Not only for the personal attacks but also for the rest of what Jessica said on the show."

"Such as?"

"Besides attacking the journal—she *knows* it's a lie—she said the House Post Office Committee is very distressed by porn publishing and is proposing—she wouldn't say anything as mild as 'considering'—a bill to raise the book postal rates. And then she talked about the journal and she and Shield both agreed its publication has to be stopped. They talked about defending our forefathers against slander."

"If the journal is untrue, it's libel, not slander. And I don't see how that charge could outlive nearly two centuries."

"Maybe they built sturdier statutes of limitations in those days."

"And who would bring the charge? What living person has been damaged?"

"Ask Jessica."

"Heaven forfend!"

When Snaith hung up, he lifted the receiver again and asked Laura to come in.

He was startled for a moment. He'd seen her in slacks at the office before, and at Marc's place Sunday night. But now he could swear she'd nothing on under that almost sheer turtleneck.

"Laura, I want to talk to Marc right away. While I'm doing it, would you draft an announcement to the press? Something simple and direct about Solus Books doing an immediate edition of the Lawrans Washington journal—let's call it *Abigail's Washington Journal*. With an introduction by Paul. Dig out the 'A' review and publicity lists. And make sure the broadcast people and news magazines are on it. Let's send it out by messenger wherever possible. Otherwise air mail. Put a note on it with this number and my home phone and say I can be reached there over the weekend. And *PW*, of course. For immediate release."

40

On Saturday and Sunday, some local radio stations carried brief items that "the journal of that Revolutionary girl from New Jersey who claimed to have had a fling with someone who sounded awfully like G. Washington" was going to be published in book form. Sunday's papers had, in fuller and more dignified phrasing, first or second news-section items to the same effect. The *Times* added the fact that Paul De Witt was writing the introduction and that he, interviewed by phone, was making no claim for the work's authenticity.

On Sunday afternoon Mrs. Laurens Lawrence phoned Paul. He listened for some minutes. "No," he said finally, "I'm not entirely happy that it's being published. Not until there's more chance to examine its truth, if any."

"Well, then? You own it, don't you?"

"So I'm told. But that's the nub of my problem. I don't think anyone should own a historical document, or even one which may be historical. Unless archives can be said to 'own' something for purposes of display or making it available in a collection."

"Still, you say you don't think—"

"I'm not sure. That's all I said. You see, the other side of the argument I've been having with myself is that some facts about it have already been made public. And that's causing conjecture—conjecture a lot wilder than the facts suggested in the text. I've finally decided to make it totally available with a warning that its contents are very likely pure fabrication. I believe that's preferable to keeping it secret while rumors build."

"But look at the damage it could do."

"To whom?"

"To Washington's memory, for instance."

"Surely you don't think Washington's memory can't withstand this rumor, or even this fact."

"It could suffer. And what sort of an example would this be. A married man carrying on with another woman!"

"What example have people been using up till now?"

"Professor! This isn't *any* married man. This is—well, really, I don't have to tell you."

"No, Mrs. Lawrence. You don't. And of course there will be

bad jokes about 'the father of his what?' Or George Washington slept *where?* But those will be forgotten very quickly."

"But meanwhile—consider the scandal." She was silent and Paul could imagine her biting her lip. "Professor De Witt. You possibly know that I'm a Daughter of the American Revolution."

"I do, indeed. John and Henry Laurens were distinguished patriots. Their services were enormous. Not only that—aren't you a descendant, at least by marriage, of James Lawrence, the battle of Lake Erie hero?"

"Yes. But that was only the War of 1812."

"Still," Paul mused, "the fact that Lake Erie is now dirty hasn't—"

"What? I can't hear you."

"Nothing. I was wandering. You were saying about the D.A.R.?"

"Yes. There was a regional meeting in New York last week. They're very upset about this journal. This morning I had another call. They—we simply can't allow it to be published."

"I don't see how you—they—can prevent it."

"Other groups have been in touch with them. By phone. Veterans organizations, some pretty powerful political groups, a senator from—well, from a very nearby state. One of Ohio's congressmen who is quite influential with—"

"Joshua Tobler?"

"Yes. And of course the whole Americans for Clean Entertainment membership. And Youth for Decency. And that group in New York—up on the East Side, in Yorkville. And some of those big Hollywood people who are so active for the Republicans right now . . ."

"That's quite a large—collection."

"Yes. The phones have been kept very busy. And a number of these people, at least the leaders, will be getting together in a day or so."

"Ah"—Paul put on a great sound of naïveté—"and you're calling to ask me to talk to them? To tell them why I think suppression of the journal would create more of a sensation than publishing it?"

"Oh, no. I don't think that would be—"

"I know. You think it's an imposition to ask. I wouldn't mind. Meeting your group would—ah, give me a great sense of the past. I'm a historian, you know."

"Well, of course I know. But, Professor De Witt, you *know* that I have great respect for you and I certainly enjoy sitting on the Library Board with you. But many of the people in the organizations I was talking about don't really know you. And some of them think you're—well, pretty left-wing."

"If that were true, it would help balance their own position. Keep them from side-slipping, you know."

"Oh, I don't—I don't really think—" She was flustered and searching for a change of subject. She found it. "I hope you will be at the special Library Board meeting tomorrow evening."

"Yes, of course. Morley Oliver called me. What can you tell me about it?"

"Professor. It's really embarrassing to discuss it. But we're going to have to at the meeting. So—you know what Hester Morehouse said on the Steve Molding show Monday night. I don't usually listen to it, it's not my idea of entertainment. But when I heard it would be all about the trial here and the journal you found . . . Anyhow, I was deeply shocked." She took a long breath. "And Tuesday morning I heard from two other members of the board who were just as upset and felt as I do that Hester should be censured. We called Morley Oliver as chairman of the Library Board and told him we wanted a special meeting."

"But what shocked you?"

"Why, Professor! Those dreadful words she used."

"But all you could have heard were bleeps."

"Yes. But *everyone* knew what she must have said."

"Quite so. In which case, why were you upset by hearing bleeps for words you already knew?"

"Because they're improper words. Words that simply aren't used in polite—*really*, Professor!"

"So you and two others want to censure Hester. It'll be very interesting to hear what the rest say. Morley didn't sound very enthusiastic about calling the meeting."

"I know he wasn't. But we insisted. You'd think he would have been outraged. After all, he used to be a television executive."

"Ah, yes," said Paul, "but remember, he was in educational TV. And that's almost as unregenerate as the BBC."

The next afternoon, in Snaith's office, Paul handed the photocopy of the journal to him. Snaith thumbed it quickly and passed it across his desk to Max Levin.

"You're not intending to edit it?" Paul asked with sudden concern.

Max reassured him. "My only job on this will be to see if there are any archaic words which need explanatory footnotes. And to make typographic suggestions."

"Please," said Paul, "try to avoid footnotes. Remember what John Barrymore once said about them?"

"Can't say I do."

"He said that jumping from the text down to a footnote was like getting out of bed on your wedding night to answer the doorbell."

Lincoln laughed. "He had a point."

Max said, "So I've always understood."

Lincoln ignored him and said to Paul, "So? Have you decided to take the royalties, or do you still insist—"

"I still insist. I want whatever normal royalty it earns to be split up among some people who can use it. By defending the right to publish it—it and other things."

"Such as?"

"Certainly the A.C.L.U. And, I should think, the American Library Association. What do they call their anticensorship group?"

"The Office for Intellectual Freedom," Snaith answered.

"That's right. And your publishing association . . ."

"They have a Freedom to Read Committee."

"Yes," said Paul. "And the Authors League. We've a censorship committee, too. You can just split the royalty into tax-exempt donations among them. And be sure it doesn't go through me to them. I'm not paying any tax on it. And, Lincoln, I may want you to give something to the Mansfield library. That will depend on how a new controversy over there comes out."

"Controversy? About Hester again?"

"Yes."

"What's she done now?"

"You ought to know, Lincoln. You were there, too."

"You mean on the Molding show—those bleeped words."

Paul nodded. "The Library Board is having her up on the carpet tonight. I'll do my best in her behalf. But the opposition may be tough." He rose and started for the door. Max Levin got up too. "Paul," he said as they went out of the office, "there's something you should know about before that meeting."

42

"I think," said Hester, looking around the group in the basement of the library, "that I'm entitled to know which of you brought this complaint."

"Now, Hester," soothed Morley Oliver, "let's just have a general discussion. Let's not make a trial out of it. Remember, the suggestion was merely to censure you—"

"Censure be damned, Morley! I won't let you pussyfoot. Either exonerate me, or fire me."

"Why," asked Edgar Dorman, the local merchant, "must you *always* make things so—so 'take it or leave it'?"

"Because anything in between is usually dishonest as hell."

"But remember," said Edna Lawrence, "what you said on the air—what would have been heard by millions if they hadn't mercifully bleeped you. Surely we have a right to question your judgment, or at least your taste."

"Sure you do," Hester said. "But you've no right to force your taste, or the petty, euphemistical taste of TV, on me. I used healthy and honest words. It was bad enough that some pettifogging people at the network bleeped them. But you're not going to make it worse by censuring me. Either take me as I am or leave me."

Charles Forney, the Negro labor leader said, "I'm sorry, Hester, but I don't think you should have used those words either. And I think the board should tell you so officially."

"So do I," ventured Hilda Banks.

Hester turned to her. "Hilda, if any of your first or third graders were still up when that program was on and heard those words, I'm sorry. They're probably not educated up to them yet. But I doubt they were tuned in at midnight. Surely you don't think your eighth graders and upper-school girls have to be protected by bleeps."

"I certainly don't think many of them know the words that were bleeped. Or should. That's why I think we ought to censure you."

Hester nodded sadly. "Okay. Now I guess I know. You brought the complaint. And you, too, Mrs. Lawrence." She looked questioningly at Charles Forney.

"Yes," he said, "I did too."

"That's it, then." Hester looked at Morley Oliver. "You said three."

"But," said Edna Lawrence, "I imagine others may join us."

"I'm not so sure," said Flora Gordon Wise. "I certainly won't."

"Is that kind of language commonplace in a magazine art department?" asked Mrs. Lawrence.

Flora grinned wickedly at her. "Why, we're even beginning to run pictures which show what the words stand for."

"But," gasped Hilda Banks, "you're a ladies' magazine!"

"But not," answered Flora, "*Godey's Lady's Book.*"

Paul looked up. "In other words, the *Playboys* have joined the ladies."

Morley laughed.

"Mr. Chairman!" said Edna Lawrence severely. "I don't think this is a laughing matter. When you were running WLLD, would you have allowed language like that?"

"We did, Edna, we did. True, we warned our audience that the program they were about to hear contained some frank talk. That was several years ago. Today, they might not be even that discreet."

"You mean they said words like—like—I can't even say them." And Edna Lawrence was blushing.

"Edna." Paul waited till he had her full attention. "Just consider how we're ducking around a couple of words familiar to us all. One is the precise word, the other the vulgar word for the same thing—for the female genitalia. Of course, as I told you on the phone, educational television has used those words in programs about sex and sex education, in discussions with teenagers. And it's a good many years now since there was a fuss in England because Kenneth Tynan used the commonplace four-letter word for intercourse on the BBC. Nowadays, on their talk shows, they use much of what used to be thought of as obscenities without any objection that I know of. Ever notice how, when an English author or actor gets on our TV, he—or very frequently she—gets bleeped."

"But that's England," said Edna Lawrence. "If it's not proper here, then Hester shouldn't have said it."

"Edna"—Paul was being very patient—"the people who heard those two bleeps the other night are sharply divided into two groups: those who had read or at least heard of *Lady Chatterly* and knew what the real words were, and those who hadn't the faintest idea what Hester was saying. Now, will someone please tell me how either group could have been hurt by either the bleeps or the words they covered?"

Charles Forney looked at Paul thoughtfully. "I suppose this is part of what you call freedom of expression."

"Yes, it is. I also call it simple honesty."

"But," Charles persisted, "don't you think *anything* that's said or printed is bad for people? May even be bad for people they're said about?"

Paul considered. "Yes, sometimes. You see, Charles, I'm not unsympathetic to those who, for instance, object to *Little Black Sambo*. It may be a demeaning racial portrait. But when you ban that, you're opening the floodgates of repression. Do you know that not so long ago some well-meaning people, both black and white, objected to the use of *Huckleberry Finn* in school reading programs because it used the word 'nigger' over and over again?"

"Do you like to read or hear that word?" Charles asked him.

"Not when it's used abusively. But when it's used as part of an accurate reproduction of a way of speech and thought, I certainly don't object. And when it's used in a world classic such as *Huckleberry Finn,* banning it is an act of sacrilege."

"Hear! Hear!" exclaimed Flora Gordon Wise.

Paul turned to her. "Flora, let's not leave Charles out on a lonely limb of defending purism. That, incidentally, is what censorship for the supposed benefit of some special group is called. Didn't you join in objecting to that Alec Guinness portrayal of Fagin in the English film version of *Oliver Twist?*"

"Well, you know it was anti-Semitic."

"If you ban that, then the way is theoretically open to ban a World War II movie because it's anti-German or anti-Japanese."

"But," defended Flora, "*Oliver Twist* isn't in the same literary class as *Huckleberry Finn.*

"The Merchant of Venice is."

"Who's banning that?"

"Some groups have tried to," said Paul, "here and there—from school systems."

"I think," said Edna Lawrence, "we've wandered far afield from what Hester said on TV. Why, the second word she used isn't even in *Webster's Unabridged Dictionary.* And it lists *everything.*"

"I know it's not in *Webster's,*" said Paul. "I looked it up. However, a young editor acquaintance of mine specializes in the philology of such words. He knew the derivation. It's in the *New OED Supplement.* He's seen advance proofs. He told me this afternoon that it comes from a Middle English word of Low German origin akin to a whole group of words which, in Middle Low German, began with the letters *ku*—and they all pertain to a hollow space. They're given as the true linguistic base of 'cunt.' "

Hilda blanched. Edna Lawrence struggled to her feet and marched to the stairs. Morley Oliver adjourned the meeting with the censure motion presumably tabled.

43

The adjournment left Hester angry. And rather nervous.
She wanted to know where she stood. She threatened to resign
if there wasn't a swift decision. Paul and Morley Oliver reassured her of their total support. But she remained belliger-
antly ill at ease.

That meeting had taken place on the ninth day since the
story first broke in the *Times*. And on the tenth day of what
Paul had originally thought would be a nine days' wonder, a
large meeting was held in the grand ballroom of Washington's
biggest hotel.

It included the groups Mrs. Lawrence had mentioned to
Paul plus several church organizations representing, among
them, all major denominations—plus a number of politicians
who were up for re-election and looking for public exposure.
They formed themselves, organizations and individuals, into
a large national movement, elected Congressman Joshua Tobler their national chairman and voted three national vice-
chairmen into office. One of these, naturally, was Jessica Carrol Conroy. Their name, adopted by acclamation, spelled out
their purpose: "Defend America's Founders From Slander."
Their emblem, a head of Washington bathed in radiance and
floating above a closed book slashed with an X, left no doubt
as to their source of inspiration or which goal they were defending. Their acronym, which hadn't occurred to them while
enthusiastically adopting their name, instantly delighted ir-
reverent souls from coast to coast, some of them columnists,
some stand-up comedians, all of them pleased to speculate on

whether DAFFS represented their mental condition or, as in England, the familiar plural of daffodil.

Some say it was in a liberated community in Massachusetts, others claim it began in a college town in the Northwest—but, inevitably, someone started fooling around with the last part of "daffodils" and came up presently with an unorganized organization which existed in acronym only: Don't Inhibit Legitimate Scholarship. Thus, in early September, DAFFS were opposed by DILS and suffering from insolence added to injury. Still, the whole thing might have blown over had not DAFFS instituted a campaign of letters threatening network executives and periodical publishers on or in whose media the publication of the journal was defended and/or the DILS poked their fun. It was, to the DAFFS, as though the Delaware were being double-crossed, Valley Forge handed a snow job and Mount Rushmore turned into a molehill. The most serious target of DAFFS was Tabard Press, which was making no secret of the fact that *Abigail's Washington Journal* was in type, that the size of the first printing had been increased 50 percent and that the advance review of upcoming original paperbacks in *Publishers Weekly* had classified it as nonfiction.

By late September, Marc and Laura received Paul's invitation to spend a weekend with him and his returned-from-Yucatán family. He was giving a bit of a party on the Saturday night. Rupert and Jenny were coming over from Bucks County, Hester and Jay would be there and so would Snaith, who, it seemed, found it convenient to make sure that Toni Faust attended too. Marc and Laura were delighted to accept, though a bit puzzled by a note of urgency in Paul's desire that they arrive no later than eleven o'clock on Saturday morning and by his use of the word "important" twice during his call.

By then the journal had just been published, was off to a fast start and the whole affair surrounding it had stretched into a thirty-five days' wonder which showed no sign of tapering off. It had been kept alive, partly, by an assortment of news items ranging from front page to second section, from serious to

absurd. None of this news had required stimulation by a publicity department. Some of it reflected seriously intended criticism. Some stemmed from denouncing DAFFS and jibing
DILS.

The most sobering and least Daff-like note had been struck
by an elder statesman of academia, a retired and revered
teacher and social critic, who agreed to a Sunday afternoon
network interview. "Of course I would not suppress the
truth," he had said, "nor a rumor of truth supported by reasonable supposition. But what have we here? A notebook filled
with the daily jottings of a young woman. A young woman of
unknown morals and mental state whose very existence re-
mains to be proved. A young woman who broadly hints at
romantic involvement with a man. How many young girls,
lonely, unattractive, repressed, have yearningly scribbled just
such seeming confessions?"

His interviewer said, "Many, no doubt. But not so many, I
imagine, have named or suggested a famous person."

"That may or may not be true. Most such scribblings remain secret. But," the eminent gentleman went on, "we must
remember that this was written—and I don't challenge the
scientists who say its age is established—by a young woman
(probably impressionable, perhaps hysterical) living in a dra-
matic and perilous time and amid battlefields and armies. At
such a time, in such a place, would not a girl's romantic dream
have very possibly centered on the one figure made most glam-
orous and unobtainable by his eminence and the cool distance
with which he separated himself from the common people like
herself?"

The snobbish son of a bitch, thought Paul, sitting before his
set. And was instantly annoyed by the next comment.

"You are making," said the interviewer, "the same point
Professor De Witt makes in his introduction. This may be
merely fantasy."

"But this fantasy is directed at the ultimate human symbol
of our national pride and probity."

"Abigail Lawrans could not have known that then."

"I'm not accusing her of anything but girlish indiscretion. And I'm sure she never intended her wish-dreams to be found. I'm accusing those who have published and publicized her fantasies. They have invaded her privacy, which, so many years after her death, cannot matter, but they have also spread a miasma of scandal around the man who, more than any other, represents the securing of our national liberty, the establishment of our constitutional form, and most of all, the dignity and virtue which we have been taught, and which we teach others, to admire, uphold and emulate."

Paul was invited to reply a few weeks later on the same program. "No, thank you," he said. "I've nothing to add to my statement that I consider historic conjecture a useful and stimulating companion to historic fact. Many times, the former has ultimately provided the basis for the latter. The journal has been published as even less than conjecture, merely as a starting point for it. But take the other side of the coin. Suppose we'd suppressed it. In whose name would we have done so? In the name of a nation too unstable to consider a founder's departure from moral custom? Or a nation so unsure of its own character that it doesn't dare contemplate a defect in a hero's? And suppose it all turned out to be true. Would that impeach his greatness?" He drew a deep breath. "Anyhow, who the hell would be listening to a Sunday-afternoon interview show during the World Series?"

Meanwhile, there had been:

¶The case of Mrs. Wanda Lemonds. Mrs. Lemonds taught American history in a district high school in West Virginia. Hoping to stir her students out of their beginning-of-the-fall-term lethargy, she had taken the *Newsweek* article, including Paul's brief essay, into the administration office and run off thirty-five copies on a dry duplicator. (By this action she inadvertently offended those authors' organizations and publishing companies which were still trying to preserve the sanctity of copyright, and allied herself with other groups which put the value of lowest-possible-cost education above the rights of the creator to the lawful income from his creation.) Mrs. Lemonds distributed these copies to her students with instructions to read them and to write an essay on "Why I Believe (or Don't Believe) What Abigail Wrote." Three evenings thereafter, a special meeting of the District School Board met to hear the complaints of 1) an outraged parent claiming that his daughter was being introduced to adultery in the guise of history, 2) an angry local patriot that "a pinko magazine and a Commie professor" were undermining forefatherly love, and 3) an alarmed purist who feared that Abigail's habits of spelling and capitalization would destroy modern language standards.

¶The case of the seventeen librarians. These had been identified as running libraries in various cities and towns and as having been commanded by their separate Library Boards to "put THAT BOOK on the fiction shelves or throw it out of the library altogether." These librarians (supported by the American Library Association) were standing fast even against the further and sinister imputation that many of them were believed to be approvers, or even members, of the Association for the United Nations.

¶The case of the three clergymen. The Reverend Mr. Dishart of Portsmouth, New Hampshire, along with Father Camillo and Rabbi Small from Boston, were driven to the top of Mount Washington, from which they offered up a tridenominational prayer that the people be spared from gullible acceptance of Abigail Lawrans' manifest lies. They further jointly announced a class action suit in the name of all persons, places, schools and other institutions bearing Washington's name. This suit, directed against *Newsweek*, Tabard Press and Paul De Witt, was for actual and punitive damages totaling $100,000,000. "Don't worry," Marc had said to Snaith and Paul, "I know this kind of suit. Chances are we can settle for less than half."

¶The case of the paranoid letter writer. "To the Editor: Sir, has it occurred to you that this heinous attack on Washington has been published in book form by a man whose first name is Lincoln? Need we of the Old Dominion say more? (Signed) Nuff Said."

44

When Marc and Laura arrived at Paul's late that September morning, the urgency Marc thought he'd heard in Paul's voice on the phone seemed to have translated itself into a sense of hurry. Martha De Witt Gould, who was waiting for them with her father as they drove up, turned out to be a small and dark-haired young woman who resembled her late mother's photographs and her father not at all. Her husband, Simon Gould, was hulking and bearded. The Gould children were there. Or, at least, as Paul led his party toward the enclosed porch, the children whizzed by in a blur of pigtails and tight blue jeans. It seemed that if they had stopped long enough to be sorted out and have their noses wiped, one would have turned out to be Pam, the other Dody.

Simon went into the house carrying the two small suitcases and returned with bottles of beer and a pitcher of early cider. Paul settled Marc and Laura and began to pace the porch. "The reason I especially wanted you out here before lunch is that something has come up. Or perhaps I should say may come up." Martha came onto the porch with a tray of tall glasses. "In a sense," Paul continued, "I'm consulting you,

Marc. But in another sense I'm acquainting you with some-thing you may, as Lincoln Snaith's lawyer, need to know about."

Martha, who was filling a glass, looked over her shoulder at them. "And it's all because I remembered something Dad had forgotten."

"That she did," said Paul. "When she and Simon came home, they'd already heard about the journal and where it had been found. Naturally, I told them the details, including your part in it."

"Mine, too, I hope." Laura laughed.

"That wasn't a necessary fact, but neither was it one I could conceal from this impudent chick."

"Nonsense," said Martha, "if a potential hostess doesn't get that kind of fill-in, how would she know how many guest rooms to prepare?"

"Damn good point," said Marc.

"We could show you one we're used to," Laura added.

"The children are in that one now," said Martha.

"How about one where it nearly started?"

"There's no bed in that one at the moment."

Marc was alarmed. "You mean it had to be destroyed?"

"Not at all," said Paul. "Mr. Allderdyce of Messrs. Allder-dyce and Winthrop, Cabinetmakers and Antique Restorers, trucked it down this morning to his shop in New Brunswick for repair. But, getting back to Martha's memory. She recalled that her mother kept a file of papers bearing on her antique purchases. And, what's more, she knew where they'd been stored after her death."

"If I hadn't remembered it," Martha said, "I'd still have looked in the attic for a marked carton. Where else?"

"Why were you looking?" asked Laura.

"Because Dad and Harry Chayne were trying to trace the bed's origin. I thought they might get a start if they knew the previous owner."

"And you found who it was?" asked Marc.

"I'm afraid so," Paul answered.

"Oh. Afraid?"

"Let me give it to you in order. Martha found the canceled check attached to a receipted bill fully describing the bed. The check was made out to Garth Flod. And Flod had signed the receipt."

"Garth?" said Marc. "Flod?"

"Yes," said Paul. "I quite agree. It's an unlikely name. However, I'm depressed to inform you that it turned out to be the least unlikely thing about him."

"Then you've found him."

"Umm. We knew the bed had been bought at an auction in this area. And both Martha and I recalled that it was from someone who was moving away. But to where? I reported the matter to Chayne, who passed it on to one of the graduate students working with him. She's a bright young woman who came up with the idea that Flod might have moved to somewhere else in New Jersey. And that there can't be too many Garth Flods anywhere. So, with the help of the telephone company—"

"This story gets unlikelier and unlikelier."

"I know. Nonetheless, she got the information that Garth Flod now lives on the outskirts of Trenton. He runs a chicken farm and, she subsequently told me, not until she got a whiff of the place did she realize how opprobrious a term 'chicken-shit' is." Paul paused. "Flod said he was very glad to see her, which she said she found hard to believe because he is a very sour-faced man. The minute she mentioned the bed and my name, he told her that he was about to get in touch with me."

"Then he wants to help—"

Paul lifted a restraining hand. "He had a copy of *Newsweek* there and said when he'd read the story and seen the photograph of the bed, he'd recognized it. He wanted to get in touch with me about the journal."

"Wait a minute," said Marc. "He's not trying to claim that it's his property after he sold—"

"No. Not exactly. He made a different sort of claim. And when I heard about it, I thought I'd better get you right down here. Because he's coming over"—Paul looked at his wrist—"any minute, now."

"But what kind of claim can he make?"

"He says he's bringing proof. He says that he has some kind of record that traces his family pretty far back." Paul sighed. "The fact is, Garth Flod says he's the great-great-great-grandson of Abigail Lawrans. But, he says, not until he read the *Newsweek* excerpts from the journal did he know that he was also the great-great-great-grandson of George Washington. In other words, a bastard from way back."

45

As Chayne's graduate student had said, Garth Flod was sour-looking. But she hadn't reported that he was also very tall, wispy, almost wraithlike, and possibly quite old. As he climbed from his scarred and dented coupe and loped toward Paul, who came from his porch to greet him, he had the appearance of a man either far younger than his withered look or much older than his lanky spryness.

His conversation was as spare and reluctantly uttered as though he were a Vermonter. He came onto the enclosed porch, acknowledged abruptly Paul's several introductions, declined a beer and accepted the cider Martha offered. "This year's," he complained as he sipped it. Then he looked at Paul,

who was saying, "I guess you know these parts pretty well."
Flod grunted.

"Before you moved away," Paul tried again, "did you live
around here long?"

"Long enough."

"You like it better down in Trenton?"

"Not in Trenton. Outside. What's to like about it?"

Paul tried another tack. "Do you still collect antiques?"

"Never did."

"Still, that bed my wife bought from you . . ."

"Didn't collect that. Always in the family. Handed down."

"Yes. Your family. Was it here a long—?"

"What I came to talk about." Flod put the cider glass next
to his chair and reached into the pea jacket he was wearing.
"My lawyer"—he stressed the word—"made this photostat of
the family record page from my Bible. Told me to show it to
you." He handed it across to Paul.

"Thank you." Paul leaned back in his chair, holding the
paper to the sunlight filtering through his shade trees.

Marc rose and stood behind Paul to study the document.
After a few minutes Paul looked over his shoulder at Marc,
who raised his eyebrows and returned to his chair.

Paul said, "This seems to trace a family back to a Lawrans
named Georgia."

"That's right."

"Who, according to this, was daughter of a Georgiana and
was baptized in 1802."

"That's right," Garth repeated. "Abigail's granddaughter."

Paul waited for him to continue.

"Like it says, Georgiana was Georgia's mother. Georgiana
had to be born in about 1777–78. *She* was Abigail's daughter. By
you know who."

Paul peered at the paper. "Well. Do we know who?" He
tapped the document. "There's no mention of a Georgiana's
birth. Or of an Abigail."

" 'Course not. That Bible wasn't in the family then. Georgia got it for a wedding present when she married." He reached again into his jacket. "Here. This here's a photostat of the presentation page. Georgia married my great-grandfather, Lucius Flod." He pointed to the first photostat on Paul's lap. "They had a son, Lawrans Flod, in 1834. He grew up and had a son, Lucius Flod II, in 1862. He married Annie Garth. And in 1887 Annie and Lucius II had me."

"1887!" Paul exhaled an admiring breath. "I wouldn't have guessed you were anywhere near that old."

"Yup. Eighty-five."

"I congratulate you." Paul glanced down again at the first photostat. "Tell me, how do you connect the Georgia Lawrans named here with the Abigail Lawrans who kept the journal?"

"Stands to reason, don't it? Same last name. And where was the journal found? In the bed that's always been in our family. The bed Georgiana was conceived in. And why did Abigail name her Georgiana? It was the fancy girl's name for George."

"Of course it was," said Paul. "George—Georgia—Georgiana—depending on what sex a child of that time was and which side of the Atlantic it was born on—lots of christening fonts heard Washington or a Hanover celebrated. But tell me" —he pursed his lips for a moment—"when did it first occur to you that this Georgia and her mother, Georgiana, were related to Abigail?"

"When I read about Abigail in the papers and that magazine. Read about what she wrote in her diary. And saw the picture of my old bed. Why? Don't you believe it?"

"Let's put that question aside for a moment. Suppose you are the—" he studied the photostat again—"the great-great-great-grandson of Abigail and—whoever the man may have been. You know, by the way, that Abigail's journal never names the man?"

"Didn't have to. It was clear enough. In that magazine. The parts they printed from the journal. Had to be Washington."

"Perhaps. That's exactly what Professor Chayne is trying to determine right now. That's why his young colleague came to see you. Now, what did you want to talk to me about?"

"Money," said Garth Flod.

"Oh, I see. For what?"

Garth Flod had his answer ready. "For compensation. That story hadn't ought to have come out. Not without my permission. And I'd never have given it." He paused, as if trying to remember a phrase. "It damages my reputation."

"Being related to George Washington would be damaging?"

"Not that so much. Being descended from a loose woman."

Paul rose and paced reflectively. "I daresay ever so many of us are, if we were to search back far enough."

"But nobody's trying to make anyone else's great-great-great-grandmother out to be a whore. And in a book and everything. The paper says you're the one who sold it to be published."

"And you want part of what you think I received?"

"Dunno what you received. I want lots. For damages."

Paul returned to his chair and sat whistling almost inaudibly.

Marc said, "You know, Mr. Flod. Any damages that may have been caused were inflicted long before the book came out. They took place in the press and on the air. And quite inadvertently on the part of Professor De Witt."

Flod gazed back at him.

"I mean," said Marc, "he had little to do with it."

"I know what you mean. And *they're* going to pay me, too. Especially that magazine—whatever they call it—*Newsweek.*"

"They are?" Marc was astonished. "Did they say so?"

"They ain't said anything. They ain't heard from me yet. But when they do—like I'm telling you, they'll pay."

Paul walked over to the porch railing and leaned against it. "Mr. Flod. I don't think you've considered the possible historic importance of this affair. *If* it proves to be historic. But your claim depends upon Abigail's record being true. If Abigail made the whole thing up, or if she were writing about some other man, then you have no basis. But if Abigail's story is true, her journal becomes an interesting bit of history. And I don't think you can successfully seek damages for statements of historic fact. Of course, if it's untrue, then I should think your only claim would be against Abigail." He waited for this to sink in. Flod gave no sign of it having done so. Paul went on, "You've seen the story in *Newsweek*. But have you ever seen the journal itself? I mean the original. The very book the woman you say is your ancestor held in her hands and wrote in?"

"Nope. How would I have seen it? I never looked under that bed. Never looked under a bed in my life."

"It's on display in the Mansfield library. We could drive over there. I don't think it would be closed yet. And Miss Morehouse—she's the librarian—"

"Yeah. I remember. Second-Front Hester."

"I never heard her called that."

"You should have lived here in the early Forties. You'd have heard it. People said she was fighting the Battle of Stalingrad on North Main Street." He cackled. "So, Hester's got Abigail's book, has she?"

"Temporarily. If it proves out, it will probably go to Professor Chayne. For his collection at Princeton." Paul squared his shoulders. "I decided that. As soon as I was advised that I'm its sole legal owner."

Marc nodded emphatically.

Garth Flod shrugged. "That's as may be. But it don't make a difference so far as what I've got coming to me. And going to get."

46

Half an hour earlier, Hester Morehouse had seen the last of the Saturday morning borrowers depart. The two girls from high school who helped her out on these half-day Saturday shifts had cleared the main desk and put the strewn-about books back on their shelves. Her assistant librarian was off today, her circulating and cataloging ladies had left, and Hester, setting the night lights and the burglar alarm, locked the front double door behind her.

She'd walked a bit more than a block down West Street away from the library, when she was overtaken by the still-spry strides of Morley Oliver.

"Morning, Hester."

"Good morning, Morley. Going out my way?"

"Only for a couple of blocks. I'm heading down there." He gestured toward a side street in the distance.

"That's far enough for me to tell you. I'm beginning to make quiet explorations for another job."

"Hester!"

"Why are you surprised? I told you. Exonerate me or fire me. And I'm going to be prepared for the latter."

"But Paul and I *told* you. We're talking to the others. I'm sure we'll get a vote in your favor."

"And maybe you won't. And also, maybe I won't be happy in a four-to-three situation."

"But you like it here, don't you, Hester?"

"Sure I do. Lots of things about it. Especially the kids. And certainly you and Paul. But I'm not going to hang around if

I'm not wanted, or barely wanted." She saw his concern. "Don't worry, Morley, I'll give you plenty of notice, if the board doesn't notify me first. Meanwhile, I'm still running the library."

"Yes. Well . . . there's something I wanted to ask you, although the possibility of your leaving almost drove it from my mind. Anyhow. What sort of reactions are you getting to the journal?"

"Nothing different. Lots of curiosity. Some 'I-don't-believe-it'—funny thing, though."

"What's that?"

"Lots of the curious ones ask to borrow the paperback. They want to read the whole thing. Not just look at the original in a case. But the 'don't-believe-it' don't want to read it at all."

"Afraid it might shake their conviction, I suppose. Hester?"

"Yes?"

"I've had a few protests about the journal. I told you of some of them. The 'How can you as chairman of the Library Board permit' sort of thing." Morley Oliver searched in a pocket and came out with a notation. "Ever hear of Karl Schmidt and Sons?"

"The produce people. I've seen their trucks."

"That's right. From Newark. Schmidt—the old man— called me last night."

"I thought I heard he'd died or something."

"It was 'or something.' Couple of years ago, the firm nearly went under. Then it suddenly escaped bankruptcy and seemed to be back on its feet. Anyhow, he called. He says we've got to take the journal out of the library or there will be legal action."

"What kind. Who'd bring it?"

"It sounded crazy. He said it would be brought by patriotic groups. Like the American Frères de Lafayette, the Sons of Kosciosko and the Descendants of Von Steuben—that's where he comes in."

Hester stopped laughing. "How?"

"Schmidt is local chairman of the Von Steuben organization."

"But what has the journal to do with them—or any of the others?"

"Nothing, obviously. But he was claiming that any detraction from Washington's reputation smeared the characters of the other famous generals around him."

"He believes that?"

"I doubt it. Anyhow, this morning I phoned Jay in Morristown. He had a funny theory."

Hester waited, curious.

"Jay says that back when Schmidt nearly went bankrupt, he was rescued by a big loan from Joe Stegma."

"I know that name."

"Sure you do. And you've seen it on trucks, too. He's the big produce wholesaler down in Trenton."

Hester's eyes gleamed. "Who is also Jersey chairman of the A.C.E."

"Right."

"But how is A.C.E. tied in with the journal?—Oh. That dame from Ohio. Laura's mother. Isn't she an organizer of the DAFFS?"

"Indeed she is. Vice-chairman."

Hester reflected. "So Stegma and Schmidt are both produce dealers. But how does that tie Schmidt in with the journal?"

"Jay has a pretty good idea there, too. He says Schmidt wasn't able to repay Stegma's loan. Because the interest was supposed to be something like ten percent a month."

"My God! That's usury!"

"It's more than that. According to Jay. It's organized crime. Stegma's supposed to be near the top of one of the mobs. And Stegma is now the real owner of Schmidt and Sons. When Schmidt couldn't meet the interest, let alone repay the loan, Stegma took over control of the business."

"I didn't know—" Hester said. "Jay didn't mention it."

"I think he's just put it together. He started digging around when Schmidt got so hot on the journal." Blocks away, a wailing began to rise and fall. "Jay's sure it's Stegma behind the whole Schmidt censorship act."

Hester considered this as the wailing, now clearly a siren, came nearer. "Why should a man in organized crime be fighting pornography? And now the journal?" She thought for another moment. "Or—putting them both together—be supporting censorship?"

"I can't answer that. Jay says maybe Stegma's just going along with the whole censorship thing the way he led that police vigilante business. Or maybe—he says—it's more sinister than that."

The siren was too close for Hester to hear the last words. A police car came skidding around the corner, raced down West Street, braked with a screech and shot into the library's driveway. Hester gasped, spun, and ran back the way she'd come. Morley Oliver panted behind her. By the time they reached the building, a policeman had opened the double doors with one of a cluster of keys hanging from a loop in his hand.

As they ran up the driveway, smoke began to eddy out across the threshold.

It wasn't much of a fire. The smoke seemed to be coming largely through the broken glass of the display case at the side of the counter, and from burning sections of carpet beneath it.

"Get a fire extinguisher," the policeman said to them, and scooping up the telephone from the counter, dialed and spoke for a moment. By the time he'd replaced the phone, Hester had yanked a foam extinguisher from the wall and handed it to him. He played it into the case and over the carpet. The flames died hard. "Smells like kerosene," said the cop and released more foam.

Hester turned to Morley. "It's the journal. It's still burning."

Oliver went nearer the case and bent to pick up something from the floor under it.

"Don't touch that!" The cop called over his shoulder. "Fingerprints." Morley straightened, looking down at the object. "It's a bat," he said. "A Little League bat."

"Yeah," said the cop, "those lousy kids."

Hester's face, anguished as she watched the contents of the case burn, hardened. "Just because it's a kid's bat doesn't mean a kid did it."

"No?" The cop was scornful.

"No." said Hester. She bent down and studied the bat. "If that's the kind of thing you call evidence, why don't you go over to Yankee Stadium and arrest Bobby Murcer. His name's on the bat."

"Ah, lady. They stamp those names on to make kids think—"

"Right!" said Hester. "And some adult may have used a child's bat to make a policeman think—or maybe it was just lying around the house, handy."

The flames were out. But a fire engine had already pulled up in front of the library. Now two firemen with extinguishers and hooks, another carrying the nozzle of a limp hose, came through the door.

A bit of smoke still rose from a section of carpet, and one fireman started to hook it away from the floor. The other men surrounded the case. One of them wrinkled his nose. "Gas?" he wondered.

"Or rubber cement, maybe," said another. "What was in this?"

"A book," said Hester, "and a small typed card explaining it."

"No cloth—or fabric?"

"No."

"Well, there's cloth in there now. I'd call it like oil-soaked rags."

"Yeah, somebody smashed the case," said the cop and pointed a foot at the bat, "and put the rags in. Then I guess he tossed a match."

A fireman knelt over the bat and looked at the signature on it. He said, "They shoulda had a left-handed case."

"What do you mean?" asked Hester.

"Murcer couldn't of hit it so easy."

Morley turned to the policeman. "How did you know about this?"

"Headquarters got me on the radio. The burglar alarm was tripped in here." He pointed to a raised window facing away from the street. "Probably when someone forced that open." He turned back to Hester. "You in charge here?" He had a notebook open.

"I'm the librarian. Yes. Hester Morehouse."

"You say a book was in this case?"

"A journal. A diary."

"Was it valuable?"

"Very. It was almost two hundred years old."

"What was it worth?"

"That's hard to say. We don't own it."

"Who does?"

"Professor Paul De Witt—"

"Oh. That thing. In that magazine. And in *The Channel*."

"Yes."

"Know where I can find the professor?"

Someone in the crowd that had been gathering in the doorway said, "He's coming up the walk now." The speaker turned. "Hey, Professor! They want to talk to you in here."

The crowd parted to allow the De Witt party to single-file into the library. Paul, Marc, Laura, Garth Flod. Then Simon and Martha shepherding Pam and Dody.

Paul crossed to Hester, who nodded toward the case. He stared down into it at the charred remnants.

Hester murmured. "A little one-book Alexandria."

"At least," said Paul, "we've copies."

"But will Chayne be able to prove anything now?"

Paul sighed. "Fortunately he was through with his physical proof."

"So burning this was purposeless." It was another woman's voice. Paul looked up and into the face of Annie Semple. "Have you a statement, Paul?"

"Not really." He gestured toward the case. "This makes its own statement, doesn't it? And it's not even much of a news story, Annie. Books have been burned so often, before. From Euclid's *Elements* to the works of Thomas Mann."

"Now will you ever know if what this said was true?"

Paul slowly shook his head. "I don't know. Chayne's team —and many others will join in—is checking against all available records." He sighed again. "Of course, this—"he nodded toward the burned case—"will make it easier for someone to throw doubt on Chayne's contention that the journal was written in the eighteenth century. He has his chemical tests all recorded but someone could say he missed something. Remember the grassy knoll and the other doubts they threw on the Warren Report?" He looked at Annie suddenly. "Yes, I do have a statement. A very simple one. Ready?"

Annie put her notebook on the counter and poised her ballpoint. "Ready, Paul."

Paul spoke very deliberately. "What the hell's the difference?"

She looked at him wonderingly. "Is that your statement?"

"That's it."

"Can you expand it a little?"

"What's the difference?" Paul repeated. "What's the difference whether Washington did or didn't stray from Martha's bed? Does the possibility of his having done so threaten us to the point where it's necessary to destroy an unproven account of it? And if it were proven—what then? Would we have to give back Yorktown? Tear up the Constitution? Raze the Washington Monument—no, I withdraw that question before the Freudians get hold of it."

Garth Flod raised his tenor voice. "Look here, Professor, you can say 'What's the difference?' all you want. But it makes a hell of a lot of difference to me. Maybe that thing you say ain't mine any more got burned up. But what about all those copies of it all over the stores? I'm sorry the thing got burned, maybe, but my reputation's still mine. And I'm going to get paid for your damaging it."

"Mr. Flod," said Marc, "I don't think you've got any kind of case. But if you say your lawyer thinks so, tell him to get in touch with me. I'd like to hear what he has to say." Marc took a card from his wallet and handed it to Flod.

Flod, studying the card, said, "Yeah. My lawyer mentioned I might run across you. Says you've been mixed up in this thing from the beginning." He studied the card some more. "He says your law firm is always mixed up in these book things. Dirty books. Dirty movies, too."

"Just tell him to get in touch." And Marc turned away.

"You know," Flod continued, not seeming to care if anyone was listening, "folks nowadays are crazy. Everybody's reading them books. I mean the dirty ones. And going to them 'X' movies. And carrying on like it was something new." He chuckled. "Back when I was raising chickens here, I got them books when I wanted them. But they weren't out in the stores —least not the regular stores—where everybody, kids and all, could get them." He looked around him. "And they sure weren't in the library."

Hester bristled. "Where were they, then—where did you get them?"

Flod laughed. It sounded like branches snapping. "Same place we used to get films. Didn't go down to the Bijou and expect to see a blue film. No sir! Had them over at the Farmer's —" He stopped and looked craftily at the others. "Well, let's just say over at a kind of club some of us local men belonged to. Just men. No women. And no kids. We had blue films all right. Curl your hair. And you know how we got 'em?" He snorted. "Around here they thought we was just a bunch of farmers. But we was smart. We got them books and films in trade. Never once had to pay cash for 'em."

Morley Oliver spoke quietly. "I suppose you can still get them from the same man?"

Garth Flod studied him. "What makes you think so? Why do you want to know?"

Morley shrugged. "It can't matter now." He turned away again. "I was just curious."

"Well," said Flod, "maybe you're curious. But you're supposin' wrong. With all them dirty books out in the open now —" He waved his hands at the crowded library shelves as though they teemed with all the world's erotica and the pornography of all time. "There ain't no call any more for sellin' them kind of books, or renting them movies either, on the sly." He lost himself for a moment in reminiscence. "Used to call them pictures 'stag' movies. Now even the *does* can go see them!" He grinned with admiration of his wit. "Right down at the movie house."

"So your friend who used to let you fellows have them in trade," said Morley Oliver casually, "he had to fall back on his produce business and build it up big?"

Flod laughed. Then, suddenly, sobered. "Who said he was in the produce business?"

"Don't worry," said Hester, "you didn't give it away. Not much of it, anyhow. Everybody's getting to know about Joe Stegma. Why, even the D.A. is bound to hear about him sooner or later."

Flod looked at her shrewdly. "Supposin' they think they do

know something. Can't pin him for anything now. Statute of limitations—you know about that?"

"We know about that," said Marc. "What we didn't know was why he was so active with—"

"With A.C.E!" Laura was staring disbelievingly at Marc. "Could Mother have known—?"

Marc was shaking his head and Morley Oliver said, "Groups like A.C.E. don't realize how they play right into the hands of men like Stegma. The economic system of the Stegmas used to depend—among other things—on laws banning erotica. You said it in court, Paul. They want a new Prohibition era. And even though illegal porn would be small-time for them today, it would be safe and easy compared to their other rackets."

And Paul, with sad agreement, said, "Book leggers!"

"You know," Laura said quietly, "I thought I never wanted to speak to Mother again. But now I think it's my filial duty to tell her about her man in New Jersey."

48

And she did. That afternoon from Paul's home.

When she finally emerged on the side porch again, she'd been gone about ten minutes.

"Thanks for the call, Paul." She smiled ruefully. "It was a short one. I've been upstairs afterwards. Recovering."

Marc said, "She took it badly?"

"She didn't take it. She didn't believe it."

"That," said Paul, "is why people like your mother are able to be so firm. Nothing shakes them. Least of all, facts."

Marc said, "She doesn't want to believe it."

"She doesn't want to believe *me*," said Laura. "And, you know, that isn't as bad for her as believing *her* all the time was for me."

"But suppose," suggested Martha, "that the true business about Stegma got into the papers. How would that affect your Mother—her A.C.E.?"

"I don't think it would," said Laura. "Not fundamentally. She'd remain firmly opposed to what *she* doesn't think other people should read. She'd never give up her principles—or prejudices. And"—Laura's voice became more assured—"she'll never give up her national prominence." She paused before going on. "I think the word would go out to screen her associates more carefully, or at least make sure they don't get caught." Laura laughed grimly. "More powerful leaders than Mother have reacted that way. Mother's a strong-minded woman, you know."

"Of course she is," said Paul, "and it's benefited you. You've inherited her strength. I don't think you'll misuse it. And you're not likely to make the mistake I think your Mother made."

"Which was that?"

"I'm guessing now," said Paul, "but I imagine your father is a weak man."

Laura nodded slowly. "He's a placid man. He doesn't like waves to be made. And when they are, he hunts out calm waters."

"That kind of mate overfed your mother's strength. It grew on his ineffectualness."

Laura sat with her jean-clad legs stretched in front of her. Then she looked up, almost slyly. "No," she said, "I'm not going to marry that kind of man."

That had been about three-thirty and nobody was expected

much before six. Except Garth Flod. And no one knew when he'd be back. He'd returned with them to the house from the library, refused Martha's suggestion that he stay for a bite of lunch and gone off in his old coupe muttering that he'd return.

At the library Morley had agreed that he'd drop in during the evening, and Hester had confirmed that she and Jay would show. Rupert and Jenny were coming up from Bucks County with Toni and Snaith, who were with them for the weekend. Only Max was making the longish drive from New York.

When Paul first thought of the party, he'd seen it as a belated celebration of the victory in Judge Negley's courtroom and a reunion of the Molding show's panel, plus such mutual friends as Rupert and Jenny. Later he conceived it as an effort to cheer Hester out of her post-bleep blues. During that board meeting he'd been fearful that the censure motion would carry; its sudden tabling had seemed a miracle engineered *in absentia* by Max. Now, with the journal burned, and the sense that some member of the Mansfield community had probably done it, he was depressed. And that was a most unaccustomed mood for Paul De Witt.

"We may catch him," the cop at the library had said.

"Or her," Hester had quickly amended.

But Paul had turned away, not bothering this time even to say, "What's the difference?"

It must have been around five when a blue panel truck stopped outside the house and a man in a neat dark suit walked up the path. Martha, coming out onto the porch, didn't recognize him for a moment. Then: "Oh, Mr. Allderdyce! I didn't know you."

"Guess you've only seen me in overalls."

"Yes. Come in."

He stood on the porch. "Your father around? I wanted to show him something. About the bed." He glanced at a small wrapped package in his hand.

"Of course," Martha said. "Dad's in his study. Come along."

More than half an hour later, Allderdyce departed. For the

next hour the house seemed empty. Martha, fussing with canapé trays, knew that Marc and Laura were upstairs changing
and that Paul was still in his study. At six-twenty she heard
Paul come out and walk toward the porch, and at the same
moment, tires crunched in the driveway. She started out to
greet the first of her guests. Who turned out to be Flod.

Striding up to the porch, he paid no attention to Martha's
conventional greeting but turned to Paul. "Professor, I got
something to say. And I'd like for that young lawyer of yours
to hear me say it."

"Of course," said Paul. "Sit down, Mr. Flod. I'll call him."
He went into the house and presently returned. "He'll be here
in a minute. May I offer you a drink?"

"Nope."

"How about trying these?" Martha was proffering a canapé
tray.

"Nope."

"Nice day for a drive," Paul essayed.

"Didn't notice."

He tried another tack. "Damn shame some vandal burned
the journal."

"Don't matter. Like I said, it's all them paperback copies of
it concern me."

"Hmmmm."

Marc, in slacks and a fresh sport shirt, came out on the
porch. Flod stood up, facing Paul.

"Professor De Witt. That's you. Right?"

"Well—of course."

"I been over to Trenton. My lawyer gave me this. Said I
should give it to you." He extended a paper to Paul.

Marc started to intervene, but Paul, taking it, unfolded and
glanced down the page. To Marc he said, "It seems to be a
'Summons and Complaint.' "

"That's what it is," said Flod. "I'm suing you and you have
to answer in court."

Two cars were pulling into the driveway.

"Excuse me," said Paul, "I have guests."

"I served you," said Flod, "and in front of a witness."

"I know," said Paul, "and I have news for you. Stick around. Enjoy yourself. I have much to tell you—and these people." He gestured toward his drive as still another car curved into it.

49

It hadn't been easy to detain Flod. But aided by some hard cider Simon Gould found in the cellar, he was kept there until everybody except Morley Oliver, who'd said he'd be late, had arrived.

By then the party was flowing freely in and out of the house, and the noise had risen enough to give Paul some difficulty assembling them in his big living room and the broad hall opening out of it. He lounged in the doorway between.

"Friends," he said, "I have something to tell you. Make yourselves comfortable." He lifted his hand and opened what appeared to be a small, black and still-dusty leather-covered book.

"This morning two craftsmen took away from here an antique bed which had been damaged accidentally. This afternoon one of them returned. It seems that in order to repair the bed—or even estimate the amount of work to be done on it— the rest of the slats, the unbroken ones, had to be removed. Within that undamaged area they found this." He held the book aloft. "A journal kept in 1777 by Abigail Lawrans."

"A copy!" someone gasped.

"By no means. This, I can assure you, is also an original. And the handwriting is identical to that in the journal we found before. I spent some time this afternoon comparing the handwriting here with the photographed handwriting in my duplicate of the other journal. The same Abigail kept it, and its ink and paper, I'm quite certain, are just as old as in the other."

Paul paused and the room remained silent. "There are immediately apparent differences between what I'll call Abigail's first journal and this second one. This one is shorter, written more hastily and with fewer dates. It's more of a narrative than a diary. However, there are *some* dates. It seems to begin in September of 1777 and continue for several months. I've deciphered most of it and I can assure you that at no time does it refer to any of the events or consequences recorded in the first journal."

"No pregnancy?" asked Jenny. "She was in her fifth month in September."

"She doesn't mention it."

"No going away to somewhere else—where Washington wouldn't see her?"

"She makes no reference to having moved."

"No lover?" asked Toni.

"Indeed, yes. There is a lover?"

"George again?" asked Hester.

"No. She doesn't refer to him. Except once when she wishes she could someday meet that august gentleman."

"My God," said Toni, "she must have been nutty!"

"But you say there *is* a lover?" Laura said.

"Oh, yes. A most ardent one. One who . . ." Paul turned to a page he had marked and searched down it. "A lover who— and I quote—'brought to our Revolution a gallant Frenchman's soldierly skills and to my bed a Frenchman's ardor.' "

"Oh no," groaned Max, "not *him!*"

"That's what the lady says," said Paul.

"But, Paul? Was Lafayette at Morristown, too?"

"Yes and no. He was there on several occasions, and he was with Washington elsewhere in New Jersey. But Abigail gives September twelfth, 1777, as the date of one of their most prolonged and athletic romantic engagements. And that was the day after the Battle of Brandywine outside Philadelphia. And Brandywine was the battle in which Lafayette took so bad a wound in his upper leg that Washington sent him to the surgeon's."

"What," asked Rupert, "could have made her invent—? It *must* be an invention, mustn't it? One story or the other?"

"Both stories must have been," said Jenny. "If the Washington affair were as real and as bittersweet as she made it sound—"

"Then she couldn't have written about a Lafayette fling as though the other one hadn't existed," said Toni.

"And if the Washington affair was an invention, then they both were." Jenny was firm.

"Why?" asked Jay.

"Because of the date—and Lafayette having a wounded leg," said Jenny. "He was probably immobilized."

"Yes," said Max, "but he *was* a Frenchman."

"Shut up, Max," said Jenny. "Abigail was obviously suffering from pseudocyesis."

"I wouldn't be surprised," said Hester. "What is it?"

"False belief in pregnancy," answered Jenny.

"Of course," said Toni thoughtfully, "the poor girl might have been a simple paranoiac."

"Probably made up these stories because she needed a father figure," suggested Jenny, "because she'd lost her real one when she was little."

"Right," said Toni. "Or else because he was around all the time and she didn't like him."

"Right," said Jenny. "Paul, is her handwriting very small, as though she wanted to be big?"

"No," said Paul, "it's on the large size."

"Exactly!" said Toni. "She was expressing her bigness."

"She probably had this kind of delusion repeatedly because she loved her own father so much," suggested Jenny.

"Or hated him, inordinately," Toni weighed in.

Paul looked from Jenny to Toni and back again. "Are you two pulling my leg?"

"Not yours, Paul," said Jenny. "I'm remembering my disasterous Psychology 203."

"And I," said Toni, "am trying to forget my half-assed stab at analysis."

"However," said Hester, "the main point is sound, I think. Abigail made it all up out of her own little Colonial head."

"Paul," said Snaith, "I want to publish this Lafayette journal, too."

"I insist on it," said Paul. "It clinches the falsity of the Washington one."

"Good thing," said Snaith, "we didn't claim that first one was true."

"Ummm. Wasn't it?" said Paul dryly.

"I wonder," said Hester, "what the DAFFS will do now."

"Start a French chapter," Max suggested.

Flod pushed himself off the wall against which he'd been leaning. "Now look here. You ain't going to print any more about my family. See?"

"Mr. Flod," said Paul, "you can't keep this out of the news. Whether anyone likes it or not, it's going to be printed."

"However," said Marc, "no one needs to know that Abigail is a member of your family . . . that you're the—what was it? —the great-great-great-grandson of a paranoiac. You're the only one claiming a relationship. And don't worry. Paranoia may not be hereditary."

Flod looked at Marc suspiciously, then at Paul. "How do I know you ain't making this whole second-journal thing up?"

Paul extended the journal toward him. "Please look this over."

Flod hesitated. "That wouldn't tell me. It might be something you had written."

"It might," Paul agreed. "However, it isn't. I suggest you or your lawyer get in touch with Mr. Allderdyce in New Brunswick. He'll tell you about finding it. And either or both of you can see this whenever you want. Meanwhile, have a drink and something to eat."

"Nope," said Flod. "Don't want nothing. But I'm going to see my lawyer again. Meanwhile"—he pointed a bony finger at Paul—"you keep hold of that paper I served on you. You hear?"

"I certainly do. And I will. I want it for my scrapbook."

Perhaps half an hour after Flod's departure, Morley Oliver arrived.

Hester was the first to tell him.

"Morley, George didn't do it."

He looked at her uncomprehendingly. "George who? Do what?"

"Washington didn't," she said. "To Abigail."

Morley absorbed this. "You make it sound as though they'd checked her for his fingerprints."

At which point Paul took over and filled him in. "So," he concluded, "Washington seems clearly off the hook."

"I suppose," Morley said, "some people will be disappointed."

"No doubt," Paul agreed. "If there weren't scandal lovers, there wouldn't be mongers."

"One person I *know* will be relieved," said Morley, "is Edna Lawrence. Incidentally, she called about something while I was out this afternoon. When I called back, she wasn't home."

"Maybe," said Paul, "you'll let me try her now. There's something in the second journal of special interest to her. I'll ask if she wants to talk to you from here. All right?"

"Sure," said Morley.

In his study Paul reached Edna Lawrence and gave her a quick rundown on the evening's events.

"There's one passage in this Lafayette journal I'm happy to tell you about." He flipped to another marked page. "Abigail appears to have written this after attending a ball at Morristown. Whether she was actually there, or merely fantasized it, we'll probably never know. However, describing the others present, she wrote:

"And then, handsome and more gallant than all the rest, John Laurens. I'd long heard of this brave Colonel and hoped that our Names, so much alike, denoted membership in a Family common to us both. But alas, after reviewing all his and my Relatives and Forbears, there was no chance that he of North Carolina was even remotely connected with my people of Pennsylvania and New Jersey.

"If you wish," Paul said, "I can furnish you with a copy of that passage. You might want to show it to your—your associates."

"I would, indeed," said Mrs. Lawrence.

"Morley tried to return your call, Edna. Do you want to speak to him?"

"Oh. Yes. Wait. Would you give him the message? It will interest you, too." And she spoke for several minutes.

When Paul returned to his living room, he searched and found Morley sharing a couch with Hester and Jay.

"Edna told me why she was trying to reach you, Morley. It was about the book-burning today."

Hester snapped. "Maybe she'd like to censure me for *that*, too!"

"Not at all," said Paul. "She was worried that you might equate her attempt to censure you with the book-burning. Her words were, 'Tell Hester I'm no Hitler.'"

"Maybe not," said Hester, "maybe she isn't a Savonarola, either. But she's sure as hell a Puritan—and they burned witches."

"It seems," Paul continued blandly, "she's so worried about guilt by association with the book burning that she wants to drop the censure move. She reached Charles Forney and Hilda Banks and they seem to have agreed."

"Hmmm, in that case I think I'll demand a vote of confidence."

"You might get it," said Paul. "The burning really seems to have pricked their conscience."

Max, standing behind him with Marc and Laura, turned around. "That's a fascinating word, 'prick.' According to the *OED*, it was used as early as 1592. Something about 'a pissing boye lift up his pricke.' "

"Good old Max," said Marc.

"And," Max continued, "it's also been used as a vulgar term of endearment."

Laura sighed. "All those wasted years back home," she said, "when I had to get along without vulgarity."

"Or endearment," said Marc.

"You know," said Laura, "they're pretty good companions."

About the Author

For some forty years, ALAN GREEN was an advertising man in the service of book publishing. He is also the author of a number of novels, one of which, *What A Body!*, won an Edgar in 1950, and two of which have just been acquired by Universal Films for television movies. He lives in Westport, Connecticut.